TIME SHIFT

By
D. J. McAllister

ISBN: 978-0-692-87715-9

Design: Dedicated Book Services, (www.netdbs.com)

DEDICATION

This book is dedicated to all the Military Members, Veterans, First Responders, and Emergency Personnel who save our lives and protect the American People on a daily basis.

Many thanks to Betty, who without her, these books would not have been completed.

If you liked this book please post a photo of this cover on your Facebook account or other social media so your friends and their friends will know where to buy this book.

AMAZON.COM / Books / djmcallister

Contents

Chapter 11   Home on The Farm 1

Chapter 12   Roy Goes to School 10

Chapter 13   This Man's Army 20

Chapter 14   Helen 26

Chapter 15   Get A Job 30

Chapter 16   Get A Second Job 35

Chapter 17   Donna 38

Chapter 18   A Very Hard Life 42

Chapter 19   Nick 45

Chapter 21   Roy Goes To School, Again 48

Chapter 22   The Military Way 59

Chapter 23   More College Days 67

Chapter 24   Get A Job 74

Chapter 25   Brenda 85

Chapter 26   Brenda Buys A Car 95

Chapter 27   Donna 100

Chapter 28   A Hard Life 106

Chapter 29   Nicholas 110

Chapter 31   Roy Goes To School, Again 112

Chapter 32   Roy Goes To College, Again 124

Chapter 33   Donna 140

Chapter 34   Blossoms 150

Chapter 35 More and More School 163
Chapter 36 Doctor Roy 173
Chapter 37 Let's Have Kids 182
Chapter 38 A Good Life. 194
Chapter 39 St. Nicholas 198

FOREWORD

Have you ever had a really bad day or experience where you said to yourself, "I wish I could go back and do that all over again and get it right this time?"

Well maybe you can.

My name is Nicholas Tanner and I'm going to tell you a story about Charles Roy Spencer. Roy was an ordinary kind of a guy, with all the hopes and dreams that everybody has. I have told this story hundreds of times and no one ever believes it.

Roy was destined for greatness even before he was born and I was designated to watch over him. I would try to help him with everything. I would whisper in his ear when there is an important thing he should do. I have to stay close to him and listen to him and all the people around him to warn him of trouble on the way.

I also watch out for Lucy. Lucy is not good and he tries to ruin every one of my assignments. It's hard to predict what people will do, but that's part of my job too. I can usually predict Lucy, so I stay alert.

I have known Roy for many years. I have followed him ever since he was born. We didn't actually meet until the day of his fiftieth birthday.

Roy had a pretty normal childhood as most kids do. He was a little clumsy sometimes, but most kids are that way. He was a little slow in school in the early years. He improved as he got older, also pretty normal.

His dad taught him everything he knew about anything Roy asked about.

He was not very athletic. He could throw and catch a ball. And run. Could he run! The one thing that he could do well was run, and fast, very fast!

He was very self-conscious, so he was not very good with girls. This is also pretty normal. But there is always one, somewhere, you just have to find her.

Because he was so self-conscious, he married the first girl who took an interest in him. It turned out to be a mistake. But I'll tell you about that all in good time.

I tried to set him on the right path, but Lucy kept interfering with everything I could do for him. Lucy is not good. Lucy also hates that name and sometimes when I get Lucy mad enough, Lucy disappears. I like that. It makes my work a lot easier.

The worst part about this whole thing, is that Lucy can look like anyone. I really have to be on my toes.

Chapter 11

Home on The Farm

Great Grandpa John Spencer and Bertha settled the land many years ago. He marked a plot of land bordering two dirt roads that came out to be 120 acres. He then registered it with the county clerk and moved in. In the last part of the 1800's, there were other settlers and farmers all around the area. Ohio was known for the good dirt and growing conditions there and farmers flocked in.

Great Grandpa spent a lot of time and money with an Artesian locating a source of water on the land and once a clean source of water was located, a well was put down. It was only a hand operated water pump that was installed in the well, but it was all there was available.

He and his wife immediately began to build a small one room house before the winter set in on them. It was a temporary house with post and beam construction and an outhouse. It took all spring and summer to cut the trees, stack the walls, saw the wood for the floors and put on the roof so they had a place to get in away from the cold. Fortunately there were many trees they could use for wood.

The fireplace was the biggest job. John was not the best mason, and they struggled to build the fireplace and chimney, but they finished it just in time. The cold weather moved in the next week. Cold weather in that part of the country, sometimes is severe and lasts a long time.

The following spring, more construction was underway and much progress was made with the house. More rooms were added, and since the house had been built near the well, a new pump was put down. A plumber was hired to build a new cistern and bring the water into the house. And someday an inside bathroom, with a tub inside the house might be added. What a miracle that would be!

During the long cold winters John and Bertha huddled together and made plans for how they would live in this new land. The first child, Jeremiah was born in June of the next year and Jacob the year after. Over the years, two more boys and a girl came into their family.

John worked day and night to build a new life for his wife and kids. He taught them everything he knew about construction and farming. He planted only three crops, corn and beans and hay for the cattle that they hoped to get.

He bought a cow at the auction in the spring. In June they would put a bull in with the cow and hope for a calf. Their first calf came in the following March and the house was filled with joy. Once the calf was big enough it would be sold for some real money. A first in their lives.

The barn was the next big project. It was also built of heavy timbers. The kids will keep it clean and put up the hay when they were old enough. Hay is an important feed for cattle, and must be handled properly. The roof leaked and you must not let hay get wet, or it might mold and then it would be no good for feed. So fixing the roof with anything he could find was the first priority. But he had to keep adding more pieces here and there to stop the leaks and tar the cracks between the pieces. It seemed to be a never-ending job, but eventually the whole roof was tarred over and all the leaks were stopped.

Over a very long time, he found and obtained several pieces of equipment. Many of the neighboring farmers were willing to sell to him some of the older used, broken, or outdated equipment that was about to be discarded for little or nothing. He had been a welder in the old country and he knew how to fix nearly everything, and he always helped anyone who asked.

Great grandpa became one of the most well liked men around town. He would do a favor for anyone who asked, if he could. This attitude continued to Roy's grandpa and his dad as well.

Over the years that Grandpa Jeremiah(Jerry) and Grandma Sarah lived there, they built additions to the house including bedrooms and a garage for an old 1922 Chevrolet four door car that he found in a ditch and towed home with his tractor. After he pounded out the dents and rebuilt the motor, the old car ran pretty good for a few years. But like most things, it finally gave up the ghost.

He planted apple and peach trees, many berry vines and had a special spot behind the house for a vegetable garden. Grandma enjoyed working in the garden and picking special things for their dinner.

The barn was soon crowded with a plow, a planter, a baler, a rake, a mower and a cultivator. All of them were in serious need of repair when he got them. He bought a welder and a tractor that didn't run very well at an auction and immediately began the needed repairs.

The tractor was an old 1923 Farmall tractor that barely got itself home to grandpa's house. But with a little maintenance, no, a lot of maintenance, it would do just fine. It took a long time to get the tractor motor and other parts rebuilt but soon he was moving right along.

Plans for an equipment shed were drawn up and work started immediately. It was important since the snow became very deep in the winter there and the equipment was being damaged by the harsh winters. The shed looked like a six car garage with two sides when it was done.

Until the '22 Chevy was fixed, Grandpa had to drive the tractor to town. The Chevy took a lot of time to finish as well. But because the Spencer's were deliberate and persistent, the work always got done, even if it took longer than expected.

During the time that grandpa Jacob (Jake) owned the farm, they found many tools, vehicles and equipment that were wrecked, in ditches, thrown away or in junkyards that they used pieces of metal for repair of other equipment. Most of the time old farm machines were just put in the fence line and trees grew up around them. It was easy enough to retrieve one with the right amount of strength, tools and determination, but it was not a fun job.

Grandpa's house was old and run down, and when he passed, Grandpa Jacob started a new house with donated wood from the neighbors and other sources that would be free. None of the wood from the tear-down was wasted, it was used to build the corn crib, and other small sheds they needed.

The new house was a whole new design. The design had two more bedrooms added and another parlor off to the side for privacy, and no second story, which meant no stairs to climb. He used concrete blocks for the basement and a new product from the brick yard called 'brickcrete'. It was the color of red brick, but the same size as a half high concrete block with two holes in it. The house looked like a red brick house from a distance. The house was extremely solid and only needed a little insulation.

The owner of the brick yard helped him out every chance he could. Blocks were only twenty cents apiece delivered, and bricks were a nickel. Jake figured that the extra charge for delivery was well worth it. Many times the guys from the brickyard would deliver for free or throw in a few extras.

It became the main chore for the younger kids to help Mom keep the house clean. One by one all four learned many things from mom. Cooking, cleaning and anything medical were very important to mom. The house was heated with wood, and that in itself was a major chore.

Most farm kids had outside chores to feed livestock and chop firewood every day. One of the chores that the younger kids had was to feed all the animals every day and milk the cow. The older kids took care of the firewood.

They had two mules, three pigs, two sows and one boar, and they would sell piglets when they were ready. They also had some cattle, and a steer. They would sell the calves when they were ready also. Last but not least, there are always a couple of dogs and cats roaming around and a milk cow.

The last things to be constructed were porches on the front and the back of the house and a lean-to shed on the barn. Mom demanded that the back porch be screened in. That took a lot of extra time and labor. But what Mom wants, Mom gets!

Jake had stopped using that very old well used 1922 Chevy 4 door and Roy inherited it through his dad. Roy welded a new floor in the trunk of the car more than once. There was also an old used 1948 Studebaker pickup truck, and that really old well used 1923 tractor that he got from a neighbor was cut up for scrap and repair parts.

Dad found a 1937 Farmall Model H tractor at the auction and he was the only one to bid on it. What luck, it ran like new! He always had to buy used tires and parts. Sometimes he would make some parts to keep everything going. It seems like every day there is regular maintenance on all of them to keep them running. But when you're broke, it's what you do.

When the cars or trucks finally couldn't be fixed, they would be set aside to be used for raw metal for the welding chores. It seemed that Roy and his dad always had some welding to do every day. The repairs never ended.

Roy had three brothers and a little sister named Elizabeth.

They all wanted to know everything that Roy knew. So he always had someone tagging along with him wherever he went. Soon they would all be in school and Roy would draw a crowd everywhere he went.

Roy and his younger brothers helped Dad build a corn crib. All they had for the crib was the old used wood from the house. They were pulling bent nails out of it and scraping and sanding it down to remove the splinters. It wasn't much, but it did the job. Now the farm seemed to be complete and working well.

During the Elementary grades Roy went to a two room school house in the Heath area until he entered high school in Newark. Once he started there, Roy walked about three miles to school and his dad felt sorry for him. Roy's dad bought him a well used bicycle when he started high school. It might not have been new, but it looked good and almost new and Roy really liked it, but Roy didn't ride it to school, there was too much chance of losing it there. Besides, he would rather run.

Roy's dad made up a punching bag out of an old Army duffel bag he found in a surplus store. He filled it with rags and hung it in the barn. Roy and his brothers and sister made use of it every day. By the time Roy was to go to high school, he had put on a lot of muscle and he could punch very hard.

Roy had a really old car that barely got itself out of its own way and around with him in it. One of the best things to happen to Roy was when a farmer down the road told him that he had an old Army Jeep made by Willys, and he would like to give it to Roy. It ran, sort of, but it had been rolled and all four fenders were crushed and the windshield was broken.

Roy's dad had found an old 1935 Plymouth four door car some years before, and it was stored out behind the barn. Roy cut the fenders off and used them to repair the jeep. Since the Jeep didn't come with a roof, Roy cut the roof off of the Plymouth, cut it to fit and welded it onto the body along with the windshield and side windows. Soon the Jeep took on a strange new look.

It took a lot of welding and scrap metal to get it running and safe. They went through it from top to bottom and repaired everything. It had a four cylinder motor that would go forever. Soon it ran like new, but looked old and a little weird. A perfect fit for Roy. But the doors were a problem, but Roy said he would figure them out later. Now it runs and keeps the rain out! It's almost comical if you are a car-guy.

Roy and his dad painted the old jeep black, put on black wall tires and recovered the seat with a nondescript home-made seat cover. It was quite a strange sight. It looks totally different now, and unless you knew your cars, you wouldn't recognize it. Even then it wasn't very obvious.

Just to make sure no one made it their own, Roy and his dad added a garage to the old house he was living in and hid the Jeep-Plymouth in it.

Then Roy was driving a four wheel drive 1935 Plymouth two door sedan with some very unusual seats and gauges, and doors that you needed to know the combination to just to get inside. But it worked for him for a long time.

Chapter 12

Roy Goes to School

Roy was the oldest of four boys and one girl in the family. Roy was an ordinary kind of a guy, with all the hopes and dreams that everybody has. He wasn't an Adonis, but he wasn't ugly either. I have told this story hundreds of times and no one ever believes it.

I have known Roy for many years. We actually met on the day of his fiftieth birthday, but I have followed him ever since he was born. He is a fascinating person. He lived with his parents in a little place outside of Newark, Ohio called Heath. Newark is a growing town and Heath is kind of a suburb.

Roy had a pretty normal childhood. He was a little clumsy sometimes, but most kids are that way. He was a little slow in school in the early years. He improved as he got older, also pretty normal.

He was not very athletic. He could catch a ball. And run. Could he run! The one thing that he could do well was run and fast, very fast!

Sometimes he would run all the way to school. He really enjoyed that because it would allow him to let out all his frustrations, and Dean couldn't keep up with him. Dean was a strong farm kid who walked the same trail to and from school with Roy.

Roy had thought about going out for football when he entered high school. He was asking one of the teachers who the football coach was. He wanted to ask about football.

One of the guys in the senior class overheard him and said, "What? You want to go out for football? You're too small! You'd never make it! Don't be silly!"

Then the big-shot senior and his friends all laughed at him and walked away. I could see Lucy close by wearing a big smile.

I'll never understand teenagers! Roy let that dumb kid shake his confidence, and Roy didn't go out for football after that. Too bad.

Roy was five foot seven and one hundred thirty pounds soaking wet, but he will grow. He certainly didn't look much like a football player. He looked like every other kid in school. He was very self-conscious, so he was not very good with girls. This is also pretty normal. He almost had a girlfriend in his sophomore year in high school, but it didn't happen.

The first thing that his dad taught him was how to use the welder and use it right. Once Roy had learned the welder, he was given the job of fixing everything on the farm that was metal. Because all of the vehicles and equipment were old and used, nearly used up, when they first obtained them, this was a recurring job.

After the welder, his dad showed Roy how to use hand tools. Starting with the hammer and saw, then all the carpentry tools and all the masonry tools. His dad built the family house with Roy's help. The littler kids would help by carrying and holding things for Roy and his dad, and cleaning up any of the scraps around the work. The old house was falling down, and something had to be done very soon.

Roy had the knack for the use of tools, and picked up the hammer his dad gave him and began to use it. He wasn't any good with it at first, but these things take time and practice.

Roy always felt like he should have a job. He found work with a neighbor down the street who had mowers, a trailer and a truck. It didn't pay much, but when you're fourteen, you don't need much.

During the years it took them to build the house, Roy received a Bachelor's Degree in Carpentry and Masonry from the University of His Dad. He learned how to frame up walls of a house. He also learned how to build a post and beam building. He understood the names and uses of everything from a crow bar to a miter box.

When he was twelve, Dad took him to a friend who made furniture, and Roy learned everything there was to learn about that part of carpentry. A Grandfather clock that Roy made out of cherry still stands in his dad's house.

He learned how to pour concrete, set forms, lay bricks and concrete blocks too. He understood the names and uses of everything from a screed to a string level. But Roy didn't want to be a carpenter or a concrete mason as a profession.

Roy could build a whole house by himself if he had the materials. He was not too good with plumbing, but electricity was easy for him.

He wanted to do something where he could help other people. He didn't know what that was, but he was sure it wasn't carpentry or masonry or any of the things that had to do with building houses.

His parents helped him as much as they could with books, encyclopedias and anything that they thought would help him with his schoolwork. He wasn't much for books, he would rather be 'hands-on' with everything he did.

So here he was, a freshman in high school, maybe a little unsure and geeky, no driver's license, no real car, and not many friends to hang out with. He had to walk three miles to and from school every day, but he had several others to walk with.

Roy's childhood was difficult sometimes. Many times Lucy got to him before I did. I'll just whisper to him from time to time until the allotted time comes and hope he listens to me.

There were a lot of mischievous and bad things going on in the school at that time. Fortunately Roy was not involved in all of them, but he did play in some of the games. Let me tell you about some of them. Starting with his freshman year.

Dean had a fount of foolishness inside him waiting to come out. Most of Dean's pranks were small and funny. Dean, however, did actually straighten up and become someone of integrity, small as it may be.

Strange as it may seem, Dean took a liking to Roy and became his protector. When an older kid would threaten Roy, Dean would tell the kid how the cow ate the cabbage, and the kid would decide he didn't want to play with Roy anymore. Dean was in the

same grade as Roy, but in Mrs. Fletcher's class. Roy
was in Mr. Walsh's class.

For some reason, young boys really enjoy making and flying paper airplanes. The boys would make
them in class and write their personal number on the
plane, then fly it out the classroom window into the
playground. The kid whose plane flew the farthest
from the window would win. All the other boys must
then pay for his lunch for that day. This happened almost every day during the school year. It was a good
thing that lunches didn't cost much back then. Roy
never did have any money. So he spent a lot of time
making a plane that would fly, really fly.

Roy put on an inch and five more pounds during the
year. Soon he will be as tall as any of them in his class.

Summer vacation was taken up with bike riding,
swimming in any water available and girls. Roy didn't
know much about girls, but he liked their looks and
their smell.

The sophomore year was less hassle but there were
still periods of craziness.

There's always one kid who is in trouble all the
time. That was Ken. He was a tall scrawny kid
dressed in jeans with half of his shirt pulled out of
his pants with all the geekyness of a fourteen year
old boy. He was smart, maybe too smart. He had
A's in all his classes, but he had been sent to the
Principal's office by all his teachers more than once.
Nearly every day.

And he knew how to get under the skin of the teachers. One day, like every other day, just after lunch, Ken was sent to the Principal's office, again.

"What did you do now, Ken?" The Principal asked.

Ken made up a whiny excuse that didn't hold water and the Principal sat him down in the outer office. Just then, the phone rang and the janitor called to get some help with a problem he found. The Principal hurried out and left Ken sitting there alone in the outer office. What a big mistake that was!

The clock in the Principal's office had the reset button on it. This button was used to synchronize all the clocks in the school after power outages and other things. The bell announcing the time to change classes was also part of the clock workings.

Orneriness overcame him and Ken climbed up on a chair and punched the button. Suddenly, all the clocks in the school began to have the hands spin around in a clockwise direction very fast. At the speed that the hands were turning, a single class would only take a couple of minutes, and the bell to change each class would ring at the designated time.

After the first bell, all the kids went out into the halls to change classes. But before all the kids could run to their new class, and all get seated, the bell rang again. All the kids ran into the halls again to get to the next class and the bell rang again. The kids quickly realized what was happening, they stopped running, and they all began to laugh.

Teachers and students were running in all directions. Most of the students were just standing in the halls and laughing uncontrollably. The Principal heard the commotion from where he was with the janitor and came running. He knew exactly what had happened, because he left Ken in his office. And who else would do a trick like this?

There were several teachers in a race toward the Principals office to get the clock turned off. After a few minutes with the bells stopped, everything began to calm down. The Principal went looking for Ken, but he had vacated the school and was not going to let anyone find him.

Roy never did see Ken again. He thought that his family moved to another town, or that his parents put him in a different school. Well, he was partly right. His parents put him in Reform School. Ken stayed there until he was eighteen before he got out.

Ken took the hint that his parents gave him and worked very hard to find an occupation that he would like. He dabbled with all the tradesmen in and around town until he came across Mr. Elmer Austin.

Elmer made and repaired clocks and watches. It was very intricate work and took a lot of hand to eye coordination and concentration. Ken finally put his mind to it and, after a few years of study, mastered it. Ken is living and working on Memphis now, where his past is unknown to anyone.

This summer vacation was much like the last two or three. Bikes, swimming and girls. None of which were well received by the intended victim. But he kept trying. Roy was still growing. He was up to five foot eight and one hundred forty pounds by this time.

The Junior year was getting more inventive and more destructive.

A bullseye was marked on the wall where a certain teacher's head would touch when he leaned back in his chair. The kids would mark the wall where they thought the teacher's head would touch and the student who marked the closest would win the pool. Roy never found out what the pool was, so he didn't play.

The boys who sat in the far rear of the class in Biology class devised a wicked little thing. When the teacher was writing on the board, as all teachers do, one of the boys would stretch and reach one of the potted plants sitting on a ledge next to a window. He would then knock the plant off of the wall to the outside. When the pot fell it would break and all the boys in the back row would laugh uncontrollably. All those boys would get detention every time the teacher would hear them laugh. For some reason, unknown to anyone, those boys never figured out how to get out of detention.

Of course all the small stuff from previous years were still going on all around the school.

But the most ridiculous idea these boys came up with was baseball. A large piece of paper was made wet and packed into a ball. This ball was then pitched to a batter who had a school yardstick in his hands. The batter would hit the ball across the room. Then a dry piece of paper was substituted for the base runner and was sent from the batter to the other kids around the room to the bases. All of this was to be done only while the teacher was facing the board. More detention!

Roy met Helen at a fair in the park that summer before his senior year and she was nice to him. She agreed to a date and it went very well with a lot of hugging and kissing. During the rest of the summer Helen gave Roy everything he wanted and more than he thought possible. He was smitten, and she knew it. Now she had him! And Lucy loved it.

He had a growth spurt hit him that year. He put on twenty pounds and three more inches. Now he looks like someone you don't want to fool around with if you are a kid looking for trouble. Roy and his brothers practiced daily on the punching bag and they all added muscle.

I told him, "Sit right here Roy." Roy sat and waited for the ceremony to continue. The next thing Roy heard was his name being called in the graduation ceremony.

"Charles Roy Spencer."

Roy stood and walked along the prescribed route until he met Mr. Rogers standing in the middle of the stage. He took Mr. Rogers' outstretched hand with his right hand and received the cardboard tube with his left.

"Congratulations Roy."

When Mr. Rogers released his hand, he spoke his name again and Roy made his way back to his seat. He reached up and moved the tassel to the left side of his cap. He was a High School graduate! His return to his seat was a blur, but he made it. He graduated!

He was eighteen and the future should have looked bright. But he didn't have many choices, the military, working on the family farm, or a job.

Chapter 13

This Man's Army

Roy worked at his dad's farm after high school every day until his dad said. "Roy, I've got the farm under control now. George is fifteen and the others are helping a lot now. Why don't you get your military service out of the way and you could learn a trade while you're in the Army?"

Roy decided to see the Army recruiter the next day. It was a short trip downtown in his four wheel drive car to the Post Office and the recruiting offices and find the door marked 'Army'.

"Good morning, sir. My name is Roy Spencer and I would like to join the Army, if I can do anything that the Army can use." He said.

"Well son, what can you do?" He said. "Better yet, what do you really want to do?"

"All I want is a little help for me to do the right thing. My dad taught me how to weld and build things out of metal. I can fix cars and trucks, and I know how to build a house. But there's more to life." Roy said.

"Is that your car out in front?" He asked.

"Yes sir. I built that." Roy said.

"What is it? I have never seen anything like it before." He asked.

Roy explained what he had done to make himself a car out of junk.

"I think you are just what the Army is looking for! Let's start with the auto mechanics. The recruiter looked through his books to get the right MOS for each one that Roy was telling him. That would be a Ninety-one Bravo MOS." Then the recruiter wrote it down.

"Building construction would be a Twelve Whiskey MOS. And the welding and fabrication would be Allied Trades which is a Ninety-one Echo." He said. "Could you take a few tests for us so we can help sort this out?"

"Sure."

The recruiter found some tests in a file in his file cabinet and ran off copies for Roy.

It took Roy some time to finish the tests, and the recruiter to grade them.

"Roy, you did excellent on all three tests, so I think you should go for Allied Trades. It would encompass all of your skills. When did you want to sign up?" The recruiter asked.

"I want to see my girlfriend before I go, but I'm ready now. When would you want me?" Roy said.

They decided on a date and time that Roy would return to be sworn in. Roy went home singing and happy that he was going to do something with his life. He called Helen and made a date for that night. They went to a drive in movie in his crazy looking car and Helen showed him a great time. Helen promised that she would be waiting for him until he was finished with the Army.

It took most of the morning, but Roy finally got signed up and was scheduled to go to Fort Jackson for Basic and AIT. After Basic, Roy was assigned to a transportation company in Fort Benning, Georgia.

In basic, Roy was issued all of his uniforms and rank and badges. Since he was assigned MOS 91E, Allied Trades, He would do machining, welding and fabrication. Allied Trades falls under Ordinance and they wear a crossed cannons badge on their shirt. As an Allied Trades worker, Roy would be assigned to a shop or motor pool where he would help in the repair and fabrication of the Company's equipment.

One day, not long after Roy had reported for duty with his Company, the Company Commander visited the shop where he was working. He informed him that Roy might also be a HET, Heavy Equipment Transport driver or mechanic in some Companies.

The CO said, "Even though you are a Ninety-one Echo, we are short of HET drivers, so I'm going to assign you to truck number G101 as the driver. But you won't be driving unless it's a big emergency. You'll be in the shop doing the machining and the welding that you normally do."

The CO and all the Sergeants saw that Roy knew all about welding and metal work. He was known to be a valuable asset and they did not want to lose him. It seemed like at least once a week, one of the guys needed somebody to work on his car. Roy would always pitch in and help straighten things out.

After Roy had been with the Company for four months, he was sent to a short school on the base for Combat Life Saving for three weeks. Roy was first in his class and is acquiring new skills and learning how the Army works.

Every soldier in the Army must be proficient with a hand gun or a rifle. There are regular trips to the shooting range to practice and keep this sharp. Roy didn't mind the shooting practice, he and his dad had been out hunting for birds and animals for food ever since he could carry a gun.

Roy didn't make sharpshooter, or any other fancy title, but he could handle a weapon and hit what he was aiming at. That was all he, and his dad wanted, weather it was a deer or a pheasant.

Roy was well liked by the CO and all the squad leaders. He cooperated with them every time there was a problem or need that he could fix. Because of his attitude to help, he quickly made PFC. Like his parents before him, he would help anyone if he could.

Roy's friendly demeanor and his helpful actions captured the hearts of the Commander and his staff and they would help him as much as they could. Occasionally a notice of a class with a short two or three day school would show up, and the commander would send Roy as they would come along. Possibly others as well if there was space available.

One thing that Roy really liked about the Army was the mess hall. He had never seen so much food on one table before. The men in the Company would walk through the line and take all they wanted of what was there. He knew that he couldn't eat like they did or he would be too fat to do his work. Roy continued to eat as if he were home. It just tasted better. Sometimes a lot better.

Another thing that he liked a lot was his little bed. It was small but so was he. It wasn't hard like a feather mattress on a hard floor, there was a little spring in it. And he had a nice soft, warm blanket as well.

It wasn't long before Roy saw that now he has more money than he has ever had before. During the time Roy was in the Army, he sent money home to Dad every payday. He doesn't need money, he has a place to sleep, a job, food, and clothes. What more could he want? Maybe he would like a woman! But the Army didn't provide that.

He thinks about Helen a lot especially when she writes glowing love letters to him. She asks when she will see him in almost every letter. She sends photos and cookies and candy that he shares with the other guys in the Company. Roy writes back to her about once a month.

Everyone wants to be his friend, because he can help them with their car, and he usually does the job for them. One day a Private entered the shop and said that he was in Allied Trades and had been assigned to this shop. He was here to help.

During the rest of his tour, he worked with the new guy in the shop and they did everything that was handed to them. They had to rebuild more than one motor, transmission, set of brakes and several other parts of vehicles. They had to fix everything from flat tires to bent fenders.

One time the Sarge brought a radiophone in to Roy that no one in the Commo shop could get to work. It took Roy a few days to figure it out, but in the end he got it to work.

Roy let the new guy do most of the welding, fabrication and other things and watched his results. By the time Roy's hitch was up, Roy had taught the new guy all he could before he left. The most important thing that he taught him was this.

"The more good we do for others in life, the better your life will be." Roy said.

Roy thought for a long time about staying in the Army. But he knew his dad needed him to help run the farm. And because of what he taught the new guy, he couldn't get it out of his mind. He had to do the right thing and he did.

Roy finished his tour with the Army and received a discharge and went home, back to Newark and the farm. While he was gone his brothers filled the gap and took on all the work around the farm. Dad was feeling much better because of it.

Chapter 14

Helen

Helen was an ordinary girl like Roy was an ordinary guy. But she had ambition, a lot of ambition. Roy met her in high school. She was in one of his classes. Roy met Helen in his senior year at school. They hit it off very well. She was fishing for a husband, but she didn't really know what she wanted. When Roy looked her way, she went a little overboard and did everything that she could think of for him. Roy was overwhelmed by all her affection and he fell hard.

The time finally came for Roy to be discharged from the Army, and Helen was waiting for him with open arms. Helen had written to Roy very often while he was in the Service. She wanted him to remember all the intimate times they had in the summer and on the weekends during the rest of their senior year.

Now that Roy has known Helen for a few years, they are making plans for the future. The biggest problem is that neither of them has a job that pays real money. Roy works for his dad on the farm, and Helen helps her mom at home, but they are both broke.

Helen found a job at 'Lil Bear Grocery Store and one of the women there, Edna, told her all about a job opening at Dunham's Sports. Helen was an outdoors person. She liked to go to the lake and fish and hunt all around the Newark area. She thought that a store like that would be just the right place for her.

"Dunham's might be the best place for me to work." She said to herself. It didn't take her long to run down there and apply for the job. It was time for her to show someone what she knew. The manager of Dunham's store was impressed and hired her on the spot. She suddenly began to feel pretty good and even a little important.

Dunham's was a raise in pay and she knew a lot more about the products there than most of the other clerks. After she had been there a couple weeks, Helen met Cheryl. Cheryl introduced her to a multi level marketing company called CRUZER and Helen saw the possibility of making some money and not being dependent on Roy all the time. Helen signed up and began to go to weekly meetings with her new friend Cheryl. It would be her money and that's important.

One day Mister Huntley, a friend of Dad's, spent some time talking to Roy and hired him as a welder/mechanic in his shop. Roy surprised Mr. Huntley with what he knew and how well he could do it.

Roy worked on cars, trucks, tractors, and everything else that needed fixing. Mr. Huntley knew whatever came in front of him was repaired correctly and in a short time. Roy's reputation soon grew around town.

He had worked at the Huntley Welding Shop for two years, when Mister Cowan asked him if he would work for him and help them build houses. Roy hastily agreed and went to work the following Monday with a raise in pay.

Roy and Helen got married five months after he was discharged from the Army. Roy and Helen rented a little house after they were married and Roy moved out of his dad's house. Then each morning she went to her job and he went to his.

Two years after they were married, she should have been pregnant, but she wasn't. There must have been something wrong somewhere. They visited doctors and did various tests on Roy. He was given a clean bill of health by the doctors. After a few tests by the local Gynecologist, they found out that Helen could not have children. Roy was devastated! She can't have kids, medically. She didn't know this, and neither did he. He wanted kids. So did she!

They saw a different doctor, and had a lot more tests. But the new doctor said there was nothing he could do. It was a difficult thing to swallow, but life goes on, and they would have to make the best of it.

Helen quickly dove into the CRUZER life with Cheryl. There were weekly meetings in various places in town. But mostly at Cheryl's house. Helen threw herself into the new business and Roy continued to drive her there.

At the beginning, Roy would go with her just to find out what it was all about. That first day, he was sitting on a couch in the back of the room when a woman sat down beside him. She was about the same age and height as Roy. She was a thin redheaded woman, and very pretty.

"Well. Hi." She said.

"Hi. I'm Roy Spencer."

"I'm Donna Davis. Why are you back here? The meeting is up front." She said.

"I only came with my wife. She signed up for this. I'm only the driver." He said.

"I know what you mean. I came with a girlfriend, but I don't want to do this." She said. She pointed toward the crowd of women at the front of the room.

"What do you do, Roy?" She asked.

"I did my time with the Army and now I'm working at Mr. Huntley's shop and with my dad on his farm." He said. "I know a little about building houses and I'm looking for a job now."

Roy and Donna would meet at the meetings and sit in the back of the room and talk. Roy explained what he did in the Service with the rebuilding and repair of cars and trucks and motorized equipment.

Donna had two kids and she talked about them a lot. Roy could not relate to that but he talked about his work and construction of all kinds. He talked about his brothers and Liz, but mostly about their business. Each time Donna mentioned her children, Roy wished, but did not say, that he wished he was able to have children.

Helen noticed that Roy was sitting in the back of the room and talking with another woman. They looked like they were enjoying each other and Helen didn't like that at all. After the meeting she made sure to tell Roy that she would not need him to drive her to the meetings any more.

Chapter 15

Get A Job

Once his military service was completed, Roy came back to Newark and his dad's farm. He pitched in to help Dad from the first day, every day. Roy knew that Edward, the next oldest son, was graduating from high school this year and there would be a need for work to be done. Dad couldn't do it all.

Roy has been working at Mr. Huntley's shop for a while. He doesn't make much money and he has realized that he needs a real job. Something he can sink his teeth into. Something that pays enough money for him to live on.

Edward would graduate this year, then George, then Richard and the last was the baby girl, Elizabeth. Mom was always fascinated with the king's names.

Roy could do it all, but he liked framing and electrical work. They all know construction, welding, auto mechanics and animals.

Edward was the plumber and framer. Like Roy, he learned it all from his dad, and sharpened his skills in the Army. For some reason, Edward enjoyed the plumbing activities when none of the others did. They were all glad of that.

George was the heating and air conditioning expert and framer. He found a job as an apprentice with John Reese. George worked with John on every job he could and studied all the books Mr. Reese had from Ashworth College in Columbus. It took weeks and months for the knowledge to blossom in George, but he finally had it.

Since they all did framing, any building they began, went up very quickly. Each of them had a nail gun, and they knew how to use it to speed things up.

Richard was told he was the most important because he was very good with concrete and masonry. Richard had found a friend at the brickyard some time ago and agreed to become an apprentice there. With his will and pure determination, he became very good at his chosen field of work.

But Elizabeth was the brains of the family. She could add a column of numbers in her head and keep all the boys in line at the same time. She studied Finance and Accounting and was very good at it. She kept the books, all the finances and did all the banking and paid her brothers bills and their paychecks.

As soon as Liz graduated from high school she went to Denison University with a partial scholarship for Economics and a second major in Computer Science. She was the youngest, the smartest and the best looking of the kids. At least that's the way she remembers it. Then she was ready to go to work as someone who could navigate through the computer and do your taxes at the same time.

Each of the boys took turns helping Dad with the farm for a week at a time. Farming doesn't know a season. There is always something to do. And most of it is hard work. No, all of it is hard work.

As each boy graduated high school, Roy's dad asked each one if they wanted to go into the Army or work with him. They all took a short tour with the military and returned home. Each time they had acquired more skills from the work they did in the military.

Liz, of course, found a job right out of college with one of the bigger companies in town. It wasn't long before she was making as much as all the boys together. But she never said a word about it to them, nor to anyone. She opened a savings account and began putting a fair amount away each payday.

One by one, each of the boys joined the Service and got their obligation out of the way. At the same time, each of the boys took all the military schools for their chosen trades. Now they all were certified by the Army. A good move on their part.

Meanwhile, Roy was scouring Newark and all the other towns in the area for a real job. Roy knew what he could do, he just had to convince someone else of his talents.

Roy always thought that building houses out of wood that was already milled to size and shape was easy. Not like that wood they had to be using for the corn cribs and the other buildings around the farm.

Mister Cowan said that he knew Roy's dad and they had talked about getting Roy a job. He also said he would help Roy get his Electrician' License. It's time for Roy to see Mr. Cowan.

One day Roy was downtown visiting Dr. Mason and he happened to see a ring in a case in the pawn

shop window. It is a big ring. It has a full carat diamond in the center, surrounded by a circle of sparkling emeralds. That is surrounded by a circle of emerald cut amethyst, and another circle of small ten
point diamonds around the outside, all mounted in
gold.

Roy stood and stared at the ring for several minutes. He thought that it was most beautiful ring he
had ever seen. But, he had no one to give it to, and
he couldn't wear it himself, and it had to be far more
expensive than he could pay, so he walked on to his
appointment.

Every time Roy walked downtown, he would stop
and look at the ring. Finally he just had to go in and
ask the price of this magnificent piece of jewelry. He
soon found out that it was "too much for me to pay,
but it's really beautiful."

Roy was downtown to see Dr. Mason and to stop
at Mr. Cowan's office and not to be dreaming about
diamond rings. So he continued on his journey. After Dr. Mason fixed Roy's back, the visit with Mr.
Cowan went well.

Mister Cowan asked him if he would work for him
and help them build houses. Roy hastily agreed and
went to work the following Monday. Another raise
in pay.

Now that Roy was working for Mr. Cowan's company, he helped Edward get a job on the crew for
Mr. Cowan. Soon all the brothers would be working
there and polishing their skills. Roy and his brothers would be building and remodeling houses in the
area, and enjoying it.

Mr. Cowan had an office in Granville, and he wanted Roy to work there. Roy was drawn to Granville, but he didn't know why. I'll tell you more about that later. Roy agreed and soon he was driving the five miles to Granville and back in his special Plymouth.

When Edward started working for Mr. Cowan, he was sent to Buckeye Lake, about nine miles south of town on Highway 79. Edward always wanted a boat, so he agreed to work at the lake. But the lake is three miles further down the road from the town. There never was a doubt that Edward would find a way to buy a boat and float it on Buckeye Lake. The only question was when would it happen.

George went to Jackson Town and Richard went to Marne. Elizabeth stayed in and around home in Newark and Heath. She would check on each of the boys once a week, without them knowing it, just to monitor their progress.

Mr. Cowan's business took a noticeable surge forward, now that Roy and his family were working for the company and doing a good job.

Chapter 16

Get A Second Job

Over the years, each of the brothers found that he could be good at one special part of the secondary part of the construction job, the trades.

One day, Ryan Atkins, a customer of Mr. Cowan's, offered to sell his house to him. Mr. Atkins wife was gone now and he didn't want to stay in that house anymore. It needed a complete remodel, and he would sell it very cheap. Mr. Cowan didn't want to take on such a big project so he called Roy in to talk to them.

Roy and Edward agreed to do the remodel if they could get the financing to buy the house. The seller agreed to carry the house for one year with small enough payments that Roy could pay them.

Roy and his brothers discussed it and finally agreed to buy the house and do the remodel. They knew that it would be an easy sell once all the work was finished.

They worked on the house for seven weeks. It was completely changed inside and out. Wood floors were sanded, walls were torn down and moved, all the rooms were opened up and repainted. When it was done, Elizabeth had a friend who was an auctioneer come and sell the house. They counted a profit of just over six thousand dollars for the family.

After they were finished with it, the new buyer told everyone about what a good job they had done. The local newspaper even ran a story on it with pictures.

The brothers continued to buy, remodel and re-sell older houses around town. Their reputation for skilled work and fast work was soon known by everyone. Elizabeth had been doing the books for them and she could see how much they were making in this venture. She also saw that all the boys were smiling a lot more than before. And she had the Spencer's Contractor's License.

One Sunday afternoon, when they were all watching a big football game between Ohio State and Michigan, Elizabeth got an outrageous idea.

Roy had already received his license as an electrician. Edward was working on his license as a plumber, George was the heating and air conditioning genius and Richard did all the masonry and concrete. Elizabeth saw what the boys were doing for Mr. Cowan and she had a meeting with all the boys.

"Listen guys!" She said. "We are spread out all over the Newark area working for Mr. Cowan."

"Most people think of construction as one job, but the truth is that it is many jobs under one umbrella. In addition to framing the building with wood, there is electrical wiring, plumbing, heating and air conditioning, sheetrock, doors, windows, roofing and masonry." She said and pointed to each boy as she said their specialty. "And we can do it all."

"We should start our own company and not be working for someone else. We could call it 'Spencer

Construction' and I know how to get it started and where to get a loan for the initial costs. We can build and remodel anything. We should be making the money for ourselves." She said. And Spencer Construction was born.

Several years later, Roy began to write books. Instructional books. He wanted to pass on what he had learned about some very difficult subjects. The first one was a book about farming. He knew from the stories his Dad and his Grandfather had told him, a great deal about the subject. He told many stories in the book and added many comments from farmers he knew or had known. The book was filled with valuable information about farming and how to grow the crops.

Roy also told stories he had gleaned from grandpa and grandma, and their parents and neighbors about their life and what they went through to get to this country and get the farm where they live.

He didn't know where to get them published, but when his younger sister Elizabeth found a publisher in a town called Lancaster, about twenty five miles south of town, he was on his way.

Roy continued with books about how to weld, carpentry, masonry, auto body and mechanics, and house construction. Roy enjoyed helping people, and this was his way of doing it.

Chapter 17

Donna

Donna has been stopping in at Emily's house every day for coffee and a friendly chat for years. Emily and Donna were having coffee when the subject of Emily's house came up. Sam, Emily's husband passed away in a freak accident two years ago.

"Now that Sam is gone, I'd like to remodel this house and make it more livable." She said.

"You've been in this house for years. Why now?" Donna said.

"It feels too small. I want it to be more open. So I can see into other rooms." Emily said.

"There's a new construction company in town and I've heard good things from someone about them. I have their number here someplace." Donna said.

Donna dug through her purse until she found a scrap of paper with the number on it. Emily called the number and Liz answered the phone.

"Good morning, this is Spencer Construction. How can I help you?" Liz said.

"I have a job for you, I think. Could you send someone to give me an estimate?" Emily asked. She explained what she had in mind and she gave her the address and directions.

"I can have someone there at ten o'clock tomorrow morning. Is that good for you?" Liz said.

"Yes. We'll be here."

Roy kept the appointment and met with Emily and Donna at Emily's house.

"Hi. I'm Roy Spencer.

"Hi. I'm Emily Jordan, and this is my good friend Donna Davis."

Roy shook hands with both of them and when he took Donna's hand he had a tingling in his heart or chest or stomach, he didn't know which, but he could feel it. Roy held her hand for only a minute, but it affected him deeply. Her hand was warm and soft and he liked it.

"You seem so familiar. Have we met before?" He asked.

It had been a very long time since Donna and Roy sat in the back of the CRUZER meeting room and talked. He looked different now. Helen did a good job of changing his looks. Different clothes, haircut, shoes, and glasses. Helen knew she didn't have much with Roy, but she would not let him see any other woman, no matter what.

"I have the same feeling, but I can't place it right now." She said.

She was about five foot six and maybe a hundred pounds. She is small proportioned but does not look skinny or frail. Her hair is well manicured and is the beautiful red that Roy always liked. She actually looks strong. She is smiling as she is reading the Newark Advocate and listening to Emily talk about her house.

Emily explained what she wanted done to the house and Roy took notes and measurements as she talked. As they walked through the house, he noticed

Donna's voice, how she talked and how she laughed. He knew that he liked what he saw and what he heard, but he didn't know what to do about it.

Once the estimate was figured, a few days later, Roy delivered it to Emily and the contract was signed. Roy and his crew would start on the house the following Monday.

"It will take about eight or ten weeks to finish the job. This is going to be a big job. Adding a new bathroom will be the biggest part. The plumbing will take a lot of time and material. Now that we have the design finished, we can start on the demolition of all the parts to remove." Roy said.

"Is it alright if Donna and I come and watch what's being done?" Emily asked.

"As long as you two are careful. I don't want either of you to get hurt." He said.

"Thanks. We'll be very careful." She said.

"Will you be staying in the house?" Roy asked.

"No. I will stay with Donna for that time. This is the phone number and address where you can reach us." She said.

"Can you tell me if you find any problems with the house before you move on through them?" Emily asked.

"Sure.

Roy and his brothers flew into the remodel job and demo was begun. Most of the main floor had to be rearranged in order to make Emily's design fit the house. The kitchen and the bathroom are always the worst. There is more work in these rooms and the fixtures are always expensive.

Fortunately, the wood floors could be sanded, re-finished and saved. That was a big one. Because of the bathroom, the kitchen had to be demolished as well. That meant new cabinets, walls, tile and lighting. All very time consuming and expensive.

Emily and Donna would visit the house every day. Donna wanted to see Roy again and Roy noticed Donna immediately and appreciated her bearing. He liked her smile, her laugh, her beauty and especially her giggle. Donna had this certain little giggle that would erupt when she found something funny, but small.

Every time Donna was at the house, Roy would find a reason to talk to her. He found that she liked the same things he liked. They had a connection, but neither one knew it just then.

Roy felt guilty about taking the time to talk to Emily and Donna when they came to visit and inspect. He told Liz about her and they would discount one half hour from the time every day that they came. Which was every day.

Donna would meet Roy at the house every day. For some reason she couldn't stop wanting to talk to him. But she didn't know why. But I do.

Spencer Construction finished the job on Emily Jordan's house and she was extremely pleased about the beautiful work they did. That was the last time Roy saw Donna, and he was sad about that.

Chapter 18

A Very Hard Life

It's been a hard life for Roy.

He didn't want to be a welder, construction worker, or a mechanic but he was good at it. He didn't want to be a carpenter or a brick layer, either. As a mechanic, he could dope out a problem that he had never seen before. One that other guys had given up on, and Roy fixed it. But that wasn't on his list of jobs that he wanted.

He was sent to a hot wet place in Georgia and spent nearly two years there. But since Roy has a good spirit, there were others that recognized it and become his friends.

The Army wasn't so bad, but it took a couple years to get through it. After he got out, he got together with his brothers and his family and continued in the family business.

A woman entered his life. Too bad he didn't recognize the faults she had. Helen did some nice things for Roy, but most of them were designed to get something from him for her.

It seems like bad luck won't leave him alone. But I know it's not bad luck, it's Lucy.

Roy's dad had an old house that was not worth much, but that was where he lived, and he was always fixing something on the farm. It was a good thing that his dad taught him all he knew about carpentry and masonry.

Roy and his brothers built additions onto Dad's house so each of them would have their own bedroom and an extra bathroom. The house was still old and should have been replaced, but there wasn't enough money for that at the time.

Roy worked all his life in construction and he lived in a mediocre house. He was always scratching for money, but his wife, Helen, spent it all as fast as she could get it.

When the divorce happened, Helen said that she wanted the house, but since Roy was living in Dad's house, she had no claim to it. She packed everything in her '52 Chevrolet and drove away.

Much later he found out that all she ever wanted from him was his money and security, not his kids. They finally got divorced. It took a long time for Roy to even think that she would do such a low life thing to him. But he never knew her.

Roy was still working in Spencer Construction, and he continued to fill those positions for many years. Once the divorce was started he no longer had any contact with Helen's family. Funny how that works.

After the divorce, Roy remembered the woman named Donna that he had met and felt that electricity in his gut for her. Roy didn't know how to find her. He searched and searched for years, but to no avail. Too bad.

For many years after the divorce, Roy worked in the Spencer Construction Company and did anything that he could to help. He kept Dad's house looking good and he dated a few women, but with no real interest. He was single again. He didn't want another marriage, but he couldn't get Donna out of his mind.

Once he goes back in time to do it all over again, the right way, things will change for the better. I picked the right date, the right age and the right place to go to. All he has to do is listen to me and do the right thing.

I told him, "You are not losing it until you stop getting up."

He dated a woman once in a while, not one girl made him feel as good as Donna did in his memory. He prayed, he wished that he could meet this girl in his memory that had him so mystified.

Chapter 19

Nick

Roy has had a grueling life and he is about to turn fifty years old. I will meet him tomorrow and if he can say the right thing, we can repair most of the terrible things in his life.

I can't explain to you how this will happen. It is enough to say that it will, and I will be required to manage every little thing so Lucy is kept away from him.

We will retreat to the day Roy entered high school in ninth grade. One very good thing is that Roy will have memories to guide him through certain parts of his life. Memories remind us of what is important. After that part is repaired, that memory will disappear. It would be too confusing to explain to you, and besides, I'm not allowed to tell secrets.

We will meet again when he turns fifty years old. I hope I get everything right by then. This is the hardest part of my job.

"Hello, Roy, I'm Nicholas Tanner. I am here to tell you a little story. Let's have a seat, this will be a long story and you might get tired of it."

I told Roy the whole story of his life and he was shocked. He doesn't know what to do now. None of the others knew what to do either until I explained everything to them.

"You must be careful not to talk to, or listen to, Lucy. It is vital to your survival."

"Who is Lucy? I don't know anyone by that name." Roy said.

"What do you mean, you don't know who Lucy is? The guy in the red pajamas with the horns. He can look like anyone he wants, man or woman. He can also look like any animal as well. Unfortunately, I always see him as he really is. Not a pleasant sight, but I have put up with it for centuries."

No person can look at him directly, it will hurt your eyes. He will try to whisper in your ear, but don't listen to him, he lies! He is the author of all lies! He won't touch you. Don't have anything to do with him! I can see him, but I'm protected from him.

"You were introduced to Donna as Donna Davis and she was someone's wife. You talked for a short time, and someone said something funny and she laughed or giggled and smiled that big smile." I said. "Do you remember that?"

"Yes, I do." Roy said.

"Don't forget that!"

Roy wouldn't forget it. I made sure of that. Memories remind us of what is important.

"Once you say the magic words, everything falls into place. You already know what they are. You have said those words hundreds of times over your lifetime. I know, because I have heard them. Once you have said them, you will return to a time which has been pre-set for you and you will start over."

"Oh God, I wish I had married Donna." Roy said.

And there we are! Those are your magic words. And here we go again.

SHIFT!

Chapter 21

Roy Goes To School, Again

Roy was an ordinary kind of a guy, with all the hopes and dreams that everybody has. He wasn't an Adonis, but he wasn't ugly either. I have told this story hundreds of times and no one ever believes it.

I have known Roy for many years. We actually met on the day of his fiftieth birthday, but I have followed him ever since he was born. He is a fascinating person.

Roy had a pretty normal childhood. He was a little clumsy sometimes, but most kids are that way. He was a little slow in school in the early years. He improved as he got older, also pretty normal.

He was not very athletic. He could catch a ball. And run. Could he run! The one thing that he could do well was run and fast, very fast! He had talked about going out for football when he entered high school.

One of the guys in the senior class said, "What? You want to go out for football? You're too small! You'd never make it! Don't be silly!"

Then he and his friends all laughed and walked away. I could see Lucy close by with a big smile.

I'll never understand teenagers! Roy let that dumb kid shake his confidence, and Roy didn't go out for football.

Roy was five foot seven and one hundred thirty pounds soaking wet. He certainly didn't look much like a football player. He looked like every other kid in school.

He was very self-conscious, so he was not very good with girls. This is also pretty normal. He had a girlfriend in his sophomore year in high school, but it didn't last.

His dad showed Roy how to use tools. Starting with the hammer and saw, then all the carpentry tools and masonry tools. His dad built the family house with Roy's help.

Roy had the knack for the use of tools, and picked up the hammer his dad gave and began to use it. He wasn't any good at it at first, but these things take time and practice.

He always felt like he should have a job. He found work with a neighbor down the street who had mowers, a trailer and a truck. It didn't pay much, but when you're fourteen, you don't need much.

During the three years it took to build their house, Roy received a Master's Degree in Carpentry and Masonry from the University of Dad. He learned how to frame up walls of a house and build a post and beam building. He understood the names and uses of everything from a center punch to a biscuit cutter.

When he was twelve, Dad took him to a friend who made furniture. Roy learned everything there was to learn about that part of carpentry. A Grandfather clock that he made still stands in his dad's house.

He learned how to set forms and pour concrete, screed and float to finish it, lay bricks and concrete blocks too. He understood the names and uses of everything from a float to a tuck point tool. But Roy didn't want to be a carpenter or a concrete mason as a profession.

Roy could build a whole house by himself if he had the materials. Not too good with plumbing, but electricity was easy for him.

Roy wanted to do something that he could help other people. He didn't know what that was, but he was sure it wasn't carpentry or masonry or any of the things that had to do with building houses.

His parents helped him as much as they could with books, encyclopedias, tapes and anything that they thought would help him with his schoolwork. He wasn't much for books, he would rather be 'hands-on' with everything he did.

There even was talk of a tutor for a short while. The only ones they could get as a tutor were girls in the same grade or a higher grade. Roy was all for that since he was getting interested in girls by then, but it fell through.

So here he was, a freshman in high school, a little unsure and geeky, no driver's license, no car, only an old bike to get around on and not many friends to hang out with.

Roy's childhood was difficult sometimes. Lucy got to him before I did. I'll just whisper to him from time to time until the allotted time comes.

There were a lot of mischievous and bad things going on in the school at that time. Fortunately Roy was not involved in most of them, but he did play in some of the games. Let me tell you about some of them. Starting with his freshman year.

During the Social Studies class, Georgie Boy found it boring. Georgie would sit on the floor through the class and the teacher did not notice. Georgie thought all this was very funny.

Sometimes a certain teacher would lean back against the wall while teaching. One day a mischievous student removed one of the casters from the chair, and when the teacher leaned back, there was no returning to normal.

This teacher didn't like being embarrassed amid the laughter from the class, so a pop quiz was given immediately.

"There is only one question on the test. If you get it right, you get an A. If you get it wrong, you get an F. Proceed." He said. "You have five minutes." The teacher chuckled as he sat in the chair.

All of the troublemakers got F's. Funny how that works out.

Fortunately Roy had some integrity and self-control, and didn't get involved in the crazy antics that a lot of the others did.

The principal and the janitor were called and the teachers chair and the kids responsible were taken to the basement shop for repair and detention. The detention lasted much longer than the repair of the chair. The Principal and the teacher made sure of that. As I watched things unfold, it seemed like a week to me.

During all of this, Roy was studying steadily to get his grades where they needed to be so he could move on to the next grade. Roy had a study class as the last class of the day, and while the kids were doing all their crazy antics, Roy was doing his homework.

Dean had a fount of foolishness waiting to come out, but Georgie Boy was just stupid. Most of Dean's pranks were small but Georgie sometimes took it too far. Way too far! Georgie never made much of himself and is still working at a minimum wage job. Dean, however, did actually straighten up and become someone of integrity, small as it may be.

Strange as it may seem, Dean took a liking to Roy and became his protector. When an older kid would threaten Roy, Dean would tell the kid how the cow ate the cabbage, and the kid would decide he didn't want to play with Roy anymore.

Summer vacation was taken up with bike riding, swimming in any water available and hoping the girls would join them, or at least stay and talk with them. Roy didn't know much about girls, but he liked their looks and their smell. There might be some hope for him after all. There will be no studying of any kind for three months unless it is in one those subjects.

The Sophomore year was less hassle but there were still periods of craziness. The teacher for US History was Colonel Jim. His picture in his Army uniform was on the wall behind him, but none of the students would acknowledge him. This always irritated him. Because of the irritation, the class had to deal with much more homework than other classes. You would think that someone would have figured that out.

Possibly the best thing to happen to Roy was the biology lab. His partner was the most beautiful girl in school. All the other guys in the class would 'accidentally' stop by their lab table just to say "hi". She shunned all of them. While they were doing the experiments, sometimes she would get scared and put her hand on Roy or grab him. This would startle him and his brain would go into park. It always took a few minutes for Roy to get back to normal.

He didn't learn anything in that class except that he really liked her touch. He almost failed the class, and if she hadn't helped him in the finals week, he would have.

Roy found that he liked the last class of the day where he could finish his homework. That gave him time at home to work with his brothers and his dad.

This summer vacation was much like the last two or three. Bikes, swimming and girls. None of which were well received by the intended victim. But he kept trying.

The Junior year was getting more inventive and more destructive.

One day, several of the senior boys decided to see if they could play a little prank on the Principal. I was so glad that Dean and Roy weren't involved in this one.

Steve and Jack were the instigators of it. Steve had a pickup and they filled it with eight big bales of hay.

It took four other boys to help load and unload the bales. They drove them to the school at two in the morning and unloaded all of them in front of the doors to the school.

When the time came to enter the school, no one was strong enough to move the bales and enter. The Principal called the police and it took six of them to move the bales aside so the doors could be opened.

The Principal never found the boys who did the prank, but he never forgot it either.

The next year some of the same boys pulled a prank on the school again, but things didn't go as well as they had gone before. The Principal had been tipped off that something big was going to happen on Halloween night.

He enlisted the help of three of the faculty to help catch the bad actors. At three thirty in the morning, a pickup loaded with eight boys parked in the driveway next to the front doors. Each boy had a bar of face soap and a damp rag. They ran to the windows and began soaping as fast as they could. The Principal and the other teachers grabbed four of them but the others ran away leaving the pickup in the driveway. Big Mistake.

The police came and took the four kids away and a tow truck took the pickup. It had been "borrowed" from another man's driveway. But he didn't know it was taken.

Now the four boys were facing a huge 'car theft' charge. They quickly gave up the names of the others who were in on the prank under a little intense police questioning.

Four were expelled from school, and four were suspended for a month. These four would have summer school to make up the courses that they missed.

Roy and Dean were asked to help with the prank before it was started, but both of them turned it down. Maybe they are learning something in school after all.

Of course all the small stuff from previous years was still going all around the school.

Roy did meet Brenda at a fair in the park that summer and she was nice to him. She agreed to a date and it went very well with a lot of hugging and kissing. During the rest of the summer Brenda gave Roy everything he wanted and more than he thought possible. He was smitten, and she knew it. And Lucy loved it.

The worst pranks that I remember were two that happened in Roy's Senior year. I am so glad he was not involved in these.

Someone, they thought it was Georgie Boy or Dean, painted the steel handrails on the stairs leading out of the school with black paint. It was timed so the paint would be wet just before the closing bell. Everyone got black paint on their hands and some on their clothes. There was hell to pay for that one.

But the worst one of all was when someone, Georgie Boy, put a dead skunk in the heating duct late on Friday afternoon. The body laid in the duct for the weekend and by the time school was to start, no one was able to stay inside the school for more than one whiff.

The school was closed and professional cleaners were called in to fumigate the school. It took a week.

Mrs. Francis, the English teacher, stopped by at Georgie's house to tell him that there was a concern that he had been involved in the skunk incident.

Georgie came to the door with a rag soaked with tomato juice rubbing his hands and arms with it. He smelled of skunk and acted sheepishly when she said.

"Georgie, there have been rumors that you were involved in the skunking of our school. Is that true?"

Of course it was true, everyone knew it, but he denied it. And, because of the 'attack' on the school, he did not graduate and never did finish high school.

Mrs. Francis was sure that Georgie had help.

"Did Dean help you with this prank?" She asked.

"No. He wasn't even in town that day. I tried to get him to stay home and help me, but he went to Hebron with his mother." He said.

Dean was on the way out the door with Georgie until Georgie saved him. Dean had been too close to Georgie for too long, not to be suspected.

After the skunk incident, things calmed down in all the classes in the school. Most of the kids studied more because they wanted to be done with school, especially the guilty ones.

But of course, there were always those kids who felt it was their right to create chaos and confusion in the school. Most of them were also expelled and the parents were up in arms. The principal met with every parent who complained and they were shown the records of the offenses. Things calmed down after that.

The Principal was asked to meet with two very important and concerned pairs of parents.

"You may not know this, but your son and your son pulled a prank on the railroad. No one has said anything to you about it?" The Principal asked as he pointed to the two parents and their sons.

"No." Said one of the parents. "What happened?"

"These two unlocked the brake on a boxcar sitting at the railroad station near here. It rolled for several miles down the track until it hit a truck unloading produce to the grocery store in the next town. There was some damage to the truck, the produce and the building. The boxcar was unhurt." The Principal said.

The police have positive witness identifications of the two boys who did it." He said. "I am now looking at those two boys."

"I feel like someone will file charges against them soon. It may be the railroad, the grocery chain, or the trucking company, but you should be ready. This is bad." He said. "It could mean jail time for both of them."

I told him, "Sit right here Roy." The next thing Roy heard was his name being called in the graduation ceremony.

"Charles Roy Spencer."

Roy stood and walked along the prescribed route until he met Mr. Harris standing in the middle of the stage. He took Mr. Harris' outstretched hand with his right hand and received the cardboard tube with his left.

"Congratulations Roy."

When Mr. Harris released his hand, he spoke his name again and Roy made his way back to his seat. He reached up and moved the tassel to the left side of his cap. He was a High School graduate! His return to his seat was a blur, but he made it. He graduated!

He was eighteen and the future looked bright. He had many choices, college, the military, a job or something else.

Chapter 22

The Army Way

As soon as Roy graduated, he was thinking about what he could do for himself now. There was a job fair at the school during the last week of classes. Lucy got to him the same day.

"You're not going to go to that job fair are you?" Lucy said.

"Sure. I want to know what might be available for me." Roy said.

"You? Don't be silly. All they want is all the brainiacs." He said. "You're not smart enough for them."

So he didn't visit any of the companies there. Roy missed out on a good chance to get ahead. Lucy smiled.

Actually Roy was smart enough for them, but he just didn't know it. He scored one hundred thirty eight on his IQ test last year. I'm sure that was enough for any of the companies. They would have enjoyed talking to him, but he didn't give them a chance.

He kicked around all summer with his friends and family and Brenda. He learned a lot from Brenda. One of his cousins had talked to him about being in the service. He told him how he went to school after he was enlisted and he learned a new skill.

His cousin made it sound very interesting and exciting. Roy would be defending the country by being a member of the military service. It was September when Roy signed up to be in the U.S.Army.

"All of you will be going to Fort Jackson for your basic." The Sergeant said.

He went off to boot camp and his military life began. Those first few months were very important to Roy. Between marching drills and cleaning the barracks and his clothes, he took tests about everything you can think of. After a few weeks of test taking, a Sergeant called the names of a list of recruits and told them what they would be doing in 'This Man's Army'.

After all the testing was finished, the Sergeant in charge announced the findings to the recruits.

"Roy Spencer, you'll be an electronics technician." He said. "You'll be going to electronics school at Fort Gordon, Georgia right after basic training."

He called off several other names and explained where they would be taking their training. When the list of names was complete he said.

"Those of you who are not going to a school, will be done with basic in eight weeks and you're finished. Then you will be sent to your duty station." He said.

Right then, Roy decided that the Army wasn't for him. He would finish the tour of service he signed up for and get out. They had him assigned to building houses only on a smaller scale.

Signal School was eight weeks of torture. It was high school shop all over again. He had Math and Basic Electronics, then more Math and AC and DC, then more Math and Electronic Components, Amplifiers, Oscillators, Radio Receivers, and Transmitters and more math.

He learned how to use a multimeter, oscilloscope and many other special pieces of test equipment.

At least, now he understood how the radio, TV and a few other electronic things worked. He could muddle his way through a repair of something, he hoped.

The Army now considers him an expert in whatever the technician in a Signal Company needs to know.

Now that the school is over, The Officer in Charge and the First Sergeant are about to read off the duty stations that each of the students will be assigned to.

"Bailey."

"Here sir."

"Fort Polk, Louisiana."

"Charles."

"Here sir."

"Fort Gordon, Georgia."

The names went on and on until Roy's name was called.

"Spencer."

"Here sir."

"Camp Ripley, Minnesota."

If there's a worse place to be sent for duty in December, I don't know where it is. It gets very cold, and very windy. Not at all pleasant.

"Oh well, it's only for the rest of the two year assignment that I signed up for." He said to no one in particular. But now, Roy was a PFC! Wow! A private first class. That must be something good. He hoped it was.

The trip to Minnesota was a long cold ride for Roy. He was welcomed by the men in the Signal Company. They couldn't do enough for him. He didn't know it, but he was one of only two men who would be repairing the company's equipment. There was a lot of it and it was always breaking down.

When it gets very cold, like it does in Minnesota, much of the equipment that a Signal company has doesn't like to continue to run. Funny thing, the commercial radios and television sets never seem to be affected.

Every month it was something new. Telephones seemed to be the worst. Sometimes it was the same thing that they had fixed just a week or two ago on the same phone. Lucy enjoys all the headaches the bad weather brings.

Roy always felt that he was working against someone. Not just bad luck or chances. He was right, but I couldn't tell him that it was because of Lucy. I have to find another way.

Roy spent most of his days in the Electronics Shop with a soldering iron or screwdriver in his hand. He became pretty proficient with the soldering iron and repairing printed circuit boards. The test equipment he had to work with wasn't the best, but he made it do the job.

The longer Roy was with the Signal Company, the more he learned. He learned about electronics of course, but he learned about people too. Some very good lessons.

As time passed, Roy found that people are usually kind, considerate, helpful, thoughtful and gracious. But they can also be evil, mean, nasty, deceitful and vengeful.

The guys in the company helped as much as they could, but there's always one. You know the one I mean. He thinks he is better than you no matter who you are. He thinks he is smarter than you are, but he's not. He is always wrong about that and many other things as well. But that doesn't stop him from being a complete jerk most of his life.

With the exception of the jerk, the company worked very well through the winter and into the spring. Roy would do almost anything for anyone who asked. Sometimes he balked when the "request" sounded stupid or ridiculous.

The jerk wrote Roy up for disobeying a direct order and it went before the company commander for review. The CO dismissed the charge.

"It says here that you wrote up PFC Spencer for disobeying a direct order. What was the order?" The CO asked.

"I told him to stop what he was doing and help me carry a box into the supply room." He said.

"Where do you get off writing him up for disobeying a direct order from you? You ordered him to stop his work to help you? You do know that is why I put up with you around here, don't you? To carry the heavy boxes we get. That is your job!" The Captain said.

"He is a PFC and so are you! You do not have rank over him. And as long as I am the CO, you never will, Private!" The jerk just got down graded by the CO. "Now get out of my presence!" He shouted.

Several men from the company were in attendance for the proceedings and word got quickly around that the jerk got taken down a peg or two to Private. He was heard by most all of them, especially the First Sergeant, say, "I'll get you for this."

The Commander stopped him as he left the building. He had the jerk stand at attention when he talked to him.

"Private, you need to hear what I'm about to say to you. You have been a jerk from the first day you arrived here. I have put up with it because you are so young. But you have crossed the line with me. You don't give orders to another private when I have Sergeants and myself to do that. And you don't threaten anyone. We take that very personal."

"Pack your stuff! I want you off this post by nightfall. I will have someone truck you to Fort Snelling. That is all!" The Captain was yelling by this time and everyone in the company was on their toes.

The jerk saluted and walked, almost ran, to the barracks. All the men in the squad were there to see the end of the jerk. No one applauded, but there was much snickering and chuckling. Roy was liked better after that, but he still was just a PFC.

Roy worked on all the electronics they had in the company, but the CO found out that Roy also knew a lot about wood and how to work it. Soon he was building bookcases for the CO.

The last thing Roy built for the CO was a beautiful desk. There was not another one like it on the post. Roy found some walnut and some cherry boards hidden in a storeroom and a few pieces of pine for filler.

Roy thought about putting a roll-top on the desk, but that was going too far. Roy built a riser for the back of the desk with pigeon holes and a set of four small drawers across the top, with a shelf to top off everything.

The Company Commander and all the personnel loved it. Everyone wanted Roy to build them something to take home, but the CO had to stop it or he wouldn't have gotten anything done for the Army.

During most of his military duty time, he kept thinking "I wish I had done something else. Maybe I should have taken the job in construction, or that job with the lumberyard or the concrete yard in Newark."

After all the recriminations he did to himself, he finally decided that this was the best choice of what he had at the time.

When it was time for Roy to be discharged, his CO and first Sergeant spoke to him.

"You should see about further training in electronics. You're pretty good at it. You have a knack at this kind of work. I will write a recommendation for you." He said.

The First Sergeant also said that he would write a recommendation for Roy.

"I will make sure this all goes into your Two Oh One File. Somebody gave it a new name. Now they call it the OMPF. That means the Official Military Personnel Folder."

They all laughed about that.

Chapter 23

More College Days

Roy's parents talked him into going to college for anything he thought he could do. He had some classes in
electronics when he was in the Army, maybe he could
continue that course of study.

It's only five miles to Denison University from
town, he decided to drive over to the school and get
the facts for himself.

His parents agreed to pay half of the fees, which
will be just enough to get him through.

Both Roy and his parents wanted him to go
to Ohio State, but tuition and fees were too much
money and driving thirty miles back and forth every day would take time away from studying. Besides
Roy didn't have enough money to stay in Columbus
the whole time.

Roy knew that if he could get an Associate Degree
in Electronics Technology, he might have a chance
in getting a decent job. Maybe he could get a bigger,
better degree later.

Roy took a drive in his '52 Plymouth to Denison
University in Granville. Denison is only five miles
west of town. It's an easy drive, and the road is pretty
good.

The car had a breakdown on the way there. It's a
good thing there was lots of tools in the trunk and
that Roy has the know how to fix it. The old cars are

pretty easy to work on compared to what we drive now. But it takes so much time. Roy thought it might be time to find a newer ride.

Denison University is a beautiful place in the middle of Ohio in a town called Granville. It looks new and clean and scrubbed every day. Denison has a well-deserved reputation of excellence.

Roy acquired several pamphlets and books from the library that told the story of the school from its beginning. He devoured them. Now all he had to do was convince the people in charge that he should be allowed to go to school there.

He noticed that the people in Granville and Denison University were much more gracious and caring than the ones in Newark and Columbus. He hoped that was a good thing.

After he read everything about the school and the town, he decided it was time to visit the school and the administration in person. Roy drove to Granville to get a look at the college and to ask about the course he had talked to them about on the phone. Nothing is better than a face to face talk if there will be questions coming up.

Then there was a flat tire to add to the fun. It really might be time to find a newer vehicle and he had to find a place to wash up before he met with any of the people there.

The interview went well and the college agreed that they would let him select the electronics classes out of the Physics course. I whispered into a couple of their ears before Roy came to see them. That may have helped.

He had already made his selections in writing and presented them to the chairman of the meeting.

All of the faculty who were present read and examined the idea he presented. Some of the faculty members liked his idea and said they were interested in this approach to his problem. But there were a couple that were not.

One of the faculty even suggested that they would name the degree "Associate of Science, Electronics Technology." All of the faculty present agreed, except the same two, and it was done.

The only restriction was that even though Roy had previous schooling and experience in the field, the course must be at least three semesters in length, and that he must maintain a three point oh average. Roy agreed.

Roy gave them his list of the classes he had hoped to get, and the chairman said they would make it up for him. Roy forgot that this would mean there would also be Math and English included.

"Since you are an in-state student and you will be attending full time, you are eligible for the Ohio resident discount. We will contact you within ten days with our decision." She said.

Two weeks later he found a letter of acceptance from the school in the mail.

"This is the schedule for the course you have selected. The next page shows the fees for the semester for you." It said.

Associate of Science, Electronics Technology.
        1   Foundation of Computer Science
        1   Technical Communication 1

1	Electronics
1	Math
2	Introduction to Computer Science
2	Technical Communication 2
2	Electromagnetic Theory
2	English
3	Intermediate Computer Science
3	Electricity and Magnetism
3	Software Engineering
3	Programming Languages

Roy had a much better social experience at Denison than at Newark High School. None of the girls there lit his candle, but I know when there would be one soon. He doesn't know who or where she is, but I do, and so does Lucy.

Roy will be allowed to start his first semester on the first of June, and he will continue straight through until he is finished. The school said that he would receive a diploma at the graduation ceremony after his last semester.

Roy worked his tail off for those three semesters. Almost nothing could stand in his way except that old car. He watched the paper for an ad for a cheap vehicle every day.

He had to replace that sick old '52 Plymouth that he was driving and get something at least twenty or thirty years newer and with enough power to get him around town in a normal fashion. It was embarrassing!

Finally his dad found a '78 Ford Fairmont Wagon that a friend's boy had and he bought it. He almost got it for nothing. It was not much of an increase in comfort or looks, but it ran good and had good tires. It was a very clean looking white. Besides, it only cost him a hundred dollars. The Plymouth went to a guy for parts.

The Ford Fairmont was not a well-loved car by the public or the media. When it was new, someone in the media made fun of the car, and ridiculed Ford for even producing it. Sometimes the Media goes too far in their "constructive comments". Ford did a nice job of building it, but there were a few design and appearance issues that made it unlovable.

Roy and I liked it but it had a spotlight on it every day, all day long. It has one big dent in the right front fender and some other little dents and very little rust but the running gear is in good working order. And it starts every time.

The daily run from Newark to Denison was easy now. The Fairmont ran good and it was a joy to drive compared to that old Plymouth.

The first semester looks like it will be very easy for Roy. He's had math and electronics, but computer science is new, and what is technical communications anyway?

Roy had most of the subjects in the Army's school, but not to the depth that was presented here.

Computer science, math and electronics are not the easiest subjects, but Roy is relentless and persistent. He wants this schooling and he will have it or else.

Sometimes the brain in all its wisdom won't shut down and let the man have some peace. In Roy's case, everything wants to be center stage and the brain can't seem to take control.

Binary? Oh you understand binary? OK. What about octal? Oh, you understand that too? What about hexadecimal? Maybe you need a little help there?

Math. I had algebra. You mean a squared plus b squared equals c squared? Oh you got that too? Good. You even had plain geometry? It's not plain, it's PLANE. What about solid geometry. Yes it's a solid, but not that kind.

What about English? Oh, you already speak English. I must say, not very well.

Electromagnetic theory? Yes that's where North and South come together. It's what keeps the earth in the right place.

Electricity and magnetism. There's no electricity to keep the earth in place, what will we do?

Mouth keep shut, someone will hear you and then we'll all be in trouble.

Eyes, stay open. When you close, it gets dark in here and we can't keep up. Listen right and left, if you close we will all have to go to detention, and none of us want that. So pay attention. Look, now you've done it, we're going to detention.

Why won't you listen to me? I'm the brain and I know what is good for us. There is a lot of instruction coming that none of us knows anything about and Roy needs to know this stuff to graduate. So, pay attention!

Sometimes Roy's brain hurt, or it was just a headache. But Roy kept going day after day. The course was long and hard at the end for Roy, but he finished it. He was going to graduate as an Associate of Science.

I told him, "Sit right here Roy." The next thing Roy heard was his name being called in the graduation ceremony.

"Charles Roy Spencer."

Roy stood and walked along the prescribed route until he met Mr. Carter standing in the middle of the stage. He took Mr. Carter's outstretched hand with his right hand and received the cardboard tube with his left.

"Congratulations Roy."

When Mr. Carter released his hand, he spoke his name again and Roy made his way back to his seat. He reached up and moved the tassel to the left side of his cap. He was a College Graduate! His return to his seat was a blur, but he made it. He graduated!

Chapter 24

Get A Job

After college, Roy thought that he could run right out and find a job in the electronics industry. He has a degree in something now. That should be worth something. It took a lot of footwork. There he was running around the city to every possible employer. Knocking on doors, passing out resumes, interviews and more interviews.

It was getting late and Roy had been out all that day walking the beat. He stopped into an electronics parts store and began his spiel to the person behind the counter.

"Wait! Wait! You need to talk to the boss. Wait here, I'll get him." The clerk said.

The boss came out of the back and Roy handed him his resume and said. "I'm looking for a job." And before he could get another word out of his mouth, the boss said, "Come with me."

He towed Roy back to his office. "Have a seat." The boss said. "I'm Dan Miller. What can I do for you?"

Mister Miller was very excited that a real person was interested in a job in his store.

"Well, Mister Miller, I'm looking for a job." Roy said.

"What do you know about electronic equipment and their operation?" He asked.

"I was a technician in the Army." Roy said. "I studied it all in school."

"Roy, I think you are just the man I have been looking for." He said.

It only took him a few minutes to read through Roy's resume. Roy hadn't done much in his life yet. But there was a little bit in the Army.

"I think you're just the man I'm looking for." He said again. "When can you start?" The boss asked.

"Monday, I guess." Roy said.

"Great! You're hired. I'll see you Monday about eight. OK?" He asked.

"OK."

Roy didn't know it, but the boss was really hurting for a clerk who knew something about electronics. All he could find was high school kids that could work a few hours to keep the store open. Roy had knowledge, and that was valuable.

One problem for Roy was that he was required to do more selling of the electronics equipment than testing or repairing the equipment. There was a tiny little repair shop tucked away in the back. It didn't have enough test equipment or even the right stuff to do the work.

Roy knew how much power each piece of equipment drew. He knew how much power and sound each piece put out. He knew nearly everything about almost everything in the store. Except maybe, the cash register. The customers were always impressed with his knowledge of everything in the store.

He sold all sorts of electronic equipment, radios, television sets, stereos, various audio and video recorders, players and amplifiers and clock radios. Even amplifiers for musical instruments, especially for the guitar, and all the cables and wiring for everything.

The pay was good with the commissions from the equipment he sold, but it wasn't what he wanted. He wanted a career and it didn't take him long to figure out that this wasn't it.

After he finally got full of it at the parts store, a friend of his told him to see Mr. Rogers at the radio station.

On his way home, he stopped in for a visit to see Mr. Rogers. Roy walked in and the receptionist said. "Good morning. Welcome to WZNP. How may I help you?"

After he told her why he was there, she picked up the phone. "Mister Rogers, please call the receptionist." She said into the PA system.

Mr. Rogers was out on the floor and when the receptionist called his name, and he came right to her desk in only seconds. The receptionist introduced Roy and explained the reason he was there. Mr. Rogers took Roy to his office and read his resume quickly.

"Have you ever worked in broadcasting before Roy?" He asked.

"No sir, I haven't." Roy said.

"Do you understand transmitters and receivers?" He asked.

"Yes sir. I studied them in school and in the Army." Roy said.

"I'm going to give you a little test. Take this pen and a piece of that paper and draw me a schematic of a power supply used to run that television there." He said and pointed to the TV set he mentioned.

Roy took the paper and pen and it only took a minute or two to draw the schematic the man asked for.

"Good! I will give you a try. You will be responsible for keeping us on the air, and repairing some of the small stuff. Do you think you can do that?" He asked.

"Yes sir!" Roy said.

"Good! You're hired. When can you start?" He asked.

"Would today be too soon?" Roy asked.

"How about Monday? You might need your rest." Mister Rogers said and smiled at Roy's joke.

He got the job! He got the job! Roy was so excited that he ran all the way back to his new Ford Fairmont Wagon and raced home.

One thing that Roy did that was very smart, he started a savings account at his bank. He signed up to put ten dollars a week into the account. It's not much, but when he makes more, he can increase it.

Now that he has a real job, Roy is going to go looking for a little house of his own. He doesn't need much.

It took him some time to get going on the house idea. Roy asked around town about real estate agents and much to his surprise, he found one who knew him. William Denning.

"You went to school with my son, Mike. I have seen you with him several times." He said. "What are you looking for?"

"A nice two bedroom bungalow with a garage and a little yard will do fine. I don't need much." He said.

Roy and William spent several days driving around town looking at houses. Roy had to explain to William what he did and how much money he made in order to give him an idea what he could afford.

Before the week was out William found the perfect place for him. It was well within his budget, actually it was down right cheap. Both in price and in quality. It needed some work, but Roy could do all that. There was a lot of paperwork coming up. But, if it all went well, Roy would have a place of his own to live in. 123 Harris looks like a good choice.

It took quite some time. The bank must examine your credit and the money coming in and going out. They must look at your job and whether you will be working there for very long. Everything about your financial life is examined in detail. Roy passed the test and his offer on the house was approved.

Roy was about to be a homeowner!

The inspector didn't find anything seriously wrong with the house. There were several issues that could be resolved relatively quickly by a new homeowner who knew what carpentry tools were made for. And Roy did.

All the gutters were clogged up with leaves and the water was getting into the basement. Someone had brought in a load of dirt some time ago and dumped it in the exact place where the yard drained off into the alley. Now the water is backing up against the house. The inspector found three cracked or broken floor joists that can be seen from the basement.

Roy started working on his house the day after he moved in. There are two ways to go about a job like this. You could do the small jobs first and have most of it done right away, or you could start with the biggest job and work down. Roy decided on the latter.

After he fixed the items noted by the inspector, he started on the kitchen. He knew it would take a lot longer, but with the wind in his sails he would breeze through it and be done with it.

There is a particular order to building a room out of nothing, and that is what Roy had in the kitchen. Nothing. He started with the walls and ceiling. Sheetrock, mud and paint was the order of the day, every day, until the room looked presentable. A little crown molding and trim always makes everything look better.

Finally after two weeks of hard labor it was done. He rented a floor sander and took off all the nastiness on the kitchen floor. A big job, but it had to be done. One more day to stain it and one more day to poly it and he felt pretty good about his kitchen.

Roy looked through the paper and visited all the hardware stores, lumberyards and building supply stores to get a deal on cabinets. If they happened to have a sale on, that's good, but if not, you can beg, but usually it won't help. He tried everything.

One building supply store had a closeout on some lower grade cabinets made of poplar, gum and other cheaper woods. He didn't have to have the wood look, they could be painted and these would work just fine. The price was cut in half to sell them too.

He quickly went home and made a good drawing to show the store manager and they selected out all the cabinets Roy would need, tagged them and set them aside for him.

Each week, when he got paid he would pay for a few and carry them home in the back of his Fairmont. Three or four at a time, he would sand and paint them white and carefully install them.

Roy was smart enough to know that he needed water and light in the kitchen more than anything. So the heavy cast iron kitchen sink was the first to go. The base cabinets came first. He replaced the sink with a stainless steel sink that fit into the new countertop over the first cabinet he installed. The cast iron sink was taken to the scrap yard.

He put more lights and outlets in the kitchen than he needed, but he liked it.

The whole countertop on both sides of the sink was covered with twelve inch square ceramic tiles that he grouted to look like a solid surface top. He does beautiful work.

He continued around the room and installed all the lower cabinets and countertops.

Since he bought so many cabinets, the store manager gave him a break on a refrigerator and a stove. They were less expensive and white so they fit in just fine. He looked for a dishwasher, but because it was so expensive, he'll have to wait till one turns up in the paper, but he made a special space next to the sink for it in the base cabinets.

Now that all the bases are in, the big job of installing the upper cabinets and the back splash was at hand. Another two weeks of hard labor and he had a kitchen. The whole room looked like it was in the wrong house. It was a jewel.

But it's time to take a break from it and concentrate on the radio station.

A few days later, a man called the radio station inquiring about an ad to sell his dishwasher. The DJ put him on hold and yelled to get Roy. Roy picked up the phone and listened to the man's tale of woe.

Roy asked permission to go and jumped in his wagon and scooped up the dishwasher immediately. It would have been easier to haul that dishwasher if Roy had a pickup. He was thinking now and that's good.

"Wow, what a deal for a hundred bucks." Roy said to himself.

The dishwasher was installed almost before he brought it into the house. He was very excited about getting it. It made his beautiful new kitchen complete, and it was white. Roy loved it.

It wasn't a week since Roy came to the realization that he needed a pickup, that someone helped him along the way with it.

His Fairmont was stolen as it sat in the parking lot where he worked. Who would steal an old Ford Fairmont? But there was the evidence right in front of him. It was gone!

The police all scratched their heads, no evidence in the parking lot, no reason for the theft, no clues, and no theft insurance. But the police would look for the car and evidence of who and how it was stolen.

Roy had to find some wheels soon. It's back to reading the paper and walking to work, sometimes running.

Roy called everyone he knew asking about a pickup that might be for sale.

"There's a farmer south of town a mile or so who has a couple of pickups just sitting at his place. He might sell one." His friend said.

Roy called his dad for a ride to this farmer's place. The farmer said he would be glad to sell one, but they have been sitting there for a long time.

"Let's get some gas and see of one will start." Roy said.

"No! They have been sitting here too long. You'll have to open up the motor and do it right or you'll damage it beyond repair." The farmer said.

Roy and his dad went over, under and through all three trucks looking for rust and broken parts and severe wear.

The '58 Studebaker body was in the best shape and it might be the easiest and quickest to get on the road, but Studebaker parts would be hard to find. Studebaker was never a high priced car or truck, even when they were new. But a '58 could be a collector, and parts could be hard to find. Maybe not.

Dad said if they could get it to his place, they could go through it and make it pass inspection and take Roy to work.

"We'll have to tow it." Dad said. "I have a tow bar in a toolbox in my truck. Let's hook it up."

The farmer was happy to be rid of it, so he gave them the title and wished them well.

Dad towed Roy back home and they put it into the garage. After a good hour's inspection, they had a list of parts that would get it to where they wanted it.

Since the stores were closed by now, Roy would take the list to the auto parts store and pick everything up tomorrow.

Roy bought a complete gasket, ring and bearing set for the flathead engine, a carburetor kit and a tuneup set. It didn't take long to pull the engine apart and get a good look at everything.

By the time mom called them for lunch, the motor was nearly rebuilt. Once the motor is put back together, a kit must be put in the carburetor. It's pretty grimy, so it will have to soak overnight. Roy worked on it nearly all day Saturday, and installed it just before dinner.

"We'd better grease those wheel bearings or I'll have to tow you back here again sometime." Dad said.

Wheel bearings are messy, nasty, hard to handle and extremely necessary to the good operation of a vehicle. Roy did not want to do the job, but there was no one else except dad, and he already voted.

Dad had been pounding out a few dents while Roy was finishing the wheels. Now it was time for some sanding and primer.

First thing Sunday morning, Roy was up at six and getting all the necessary tools picked and set out on the workbench. Then off to church and a lot of praying for help to finish this job.

Roy was on it with his Dual Action sander, sanding every little spot. By four o'clock, it was ready for tack rags and a color coat. There's still a few wrinkles in the body, but it really looks good with white all over it.

A good vacuuming and wipe down inside and out will help clean it up. But the tires look like they won't make it around the block.

"It's going to need a grease job before we take it out. We put new oil in it when we did the motor." Roy said. "It's running pretty smooth now."

Roy was careful going to work Monday. He called Mark's Newark Tire Co. to get tires for the truck. He has known Mark for a few years. He took it to them at lunch and left it.

"Let's get white walls, it'll dress it up a little." He said.

"Nice paint job, Roy." Mark said.

On the way back to work, Roy stopped at the Courthouse and transferred the title and bought plates for it.

It's been a real hassle to get going again after the car was stolen. Roy stopped at the police station to show off his truck and to let them know who would be driving his 'new' truck.

Roy parked the truck right in front of the radio station so everyone could get a good look at it and remember where it was and who owned it.

Chapter 25

Brenda

The only girl who showed any interest in Roy during his time in high school and after graduation was Brenda. Roy didn't do well with the girls when he went to high school. He met Brenda at a fair during the summer after his graduation. They dated several times before he joined the Army. She wrote to him and sent pictures several times during his hitch. She didn't want him to forget all those wonderful things she did for him.

He was anxious to see her after his discharge.

Roy looks a few years older than he really is and Brenda looks the same age as Roy even though she is twelve years older than him and has been married, divorced and has two female children. Only he doesn't know any of this information and she wasn't volunteering any of it.

All during the time Roy was dating Brenda, he never met, or even saw the girls. Roy needs to ask more questions, but he wasn't listening to me. He had other things on his mind, and Lucy was in his ear every day.

Brenda has two girls, Cathy and Laurie. Cathy is fourteen and Laurie is thirteen. The girls hate each other for various reasons, but the most important is this. They are one year apart in age and Laurie could always get any guy she wanted, Cathy wasn't as fortunate. Lucy had influenced both girls from the beginning, but they didn't know that, and neither did Brenda.

Cathy would spend her life trying to steal any boyfriend away from Laurie by any means possible. If Laurie did actually steal a boyfriend back, Cathy would tell stories, lies, about her and the boyfriend. Making it look like Cathy had no fault in the whole affair. Tears and whining was always an addition to the story.

"Laurie lies and Cathy cries."

Cathy had a unique ability to darken a room. If there were several people in a room talking and socializing, and Cathy walked in, the talk would suddenly stop and arguing would begin. I have never seen anything like it.

The girls only wanted one hundred percent of Mom's attention one hundred percent of the time. Because of that they told lies about each other to any one who would listen. Most of the people in town have heard about the two girls and they gave them a wide berth. No one actually believes anything they say. Most people don't even want to listen to them.

But one thing they could agree on was that they hated Roy. Since the girls were continually vying for Mom's attention, anytime Roy was in the picture, they had reason to hate him. More and more every day.

But one thing the girls knew, probably because Brenda told them, was that Roy was the only one working and making enough money to support the family. They must not accuse him of any crime, especially ones that they made up, that would take him, and his money, away from them. They all agreed to this.

"If you girls screw this up for me you will find your bags and clothes in the front yard. I have found the most wonderful place for me in the world, and I won't give it up without a fight." She said.

"Don't think I don't remember all the things you two have done that hurt me. Remember the blue pickup." She said.

"OK! OK!" They said in unison.

"Where is this wonderful place, mom?" Lorie asked.

"Under Roy." She said. "I've tried it. I like it."

They didn't like that! But nothing was said.

Even though the girls said they would be good and not tell any more lies about Roy, they lied. Again. But mom didn't know that.

Since both girls knew that this marriage was coming up soon and that it would put them at a disadvantage with Mom and Roy, they made several plans about what they could, and couldn't, say about Roy.

Brenda is a sometimes clerk, sometimes shelf stocker, and sometimes supply room organizer. All of these are the lowest available jobs in the store. They pay minimum wage with a check every two weeks.

She hides any extra grocery and utility money in a savings account with only her name on it. It is in an account in another town in another state so neither the girls nor Roy will find out about it.

An accounting should be made. There are accounts in Ohio, Kansas, Colorado and Florida. Each account started very small. Ten or fifteen dollars, but over the years, they grew to hundreds. The one in Florida even has a couple thousand in it. And no one knows about it but her, not even her girls. Especially not the girls!

Laurie said Roy had a crush on the girl at the library. She said that he spends a lot of time with her when he's there. So Brenda went to the library one day just to see what Laurie was talking about.

Roy was sitting at a table studying a book, with his pen in hand, making notes on a yellow paper legal pad.

The girl at the reception desk was talking to a boy who she seemed to like. She was making all the moves that a girl makes when she talks to a boyfriend or someone she would like to assume that role.

Brenda had the good sense to bring a camera and took pictures of Roy and his note pad, and the receptionist and her boyfriend.

What Laurie had said was a lie but no one even asked about it, they always believed Laurie, even though she always lied, and every body knows it. But Brenda now knows. Strike one!

Laurie has been this way since first grade. Brenda took years to find out the reason she was like this. She found that her sister used to baby sit Laurie when she was very little. Brenda's sister lies about everything. It's almost a ritual with her. She must get up in the morning and say to herself, "What am I going to lie about today?" I've know many very important people who think this way.

It's unfortunate, but Brenda's sister rubbed off on Laurie and now it seems to be ingrained in her.

Brenda has said several times that she needed to find a car to use.

Roy said, "Why don't you look around and I'll help you get something?"

One day Roy was walking into a café, but I stopped him and told him to walk down the block and go into the pawn shop. When Roy looked down into one of the showcases he saw the most beautiful ring he had ever seen.

"Could I see that ring please?" He said.

"A beauty isn't it?' The store owner said.

"Yes. How much is it?"

The store owner quoted him a price that seemed very low, and he had enough money in his pocket to buy it. So he did. Roy and the pawn shop owner thought it was costume jewelry and that he might give it as a present sometime.

The store owner put the ring in a nice box and a little bag and Roy hurried down the street to a fancy jewelry store two blocks away.

Roy walked quickly to Taylor Jewelry and hurried into the store. Taylor Jewelry has a reputation for being very fair and very intelligent about their business. He showed the ring to the jeweler who looked shocked when he saw it.

"Could you tell me anything about this ring?" Roy asked.

"Where did you find this?" He asked.

"In a pawn shop." Roy said.

It is a big ring. It has a full carat diamond in the center, surrounded by a circle of sparkling emeralds, that is surrounded by a circle of emerald cut amethyst, and a circle of small ten point diamonds around the outside, all mounted in gold.

"This is some very fine work and the jewels here are special, this is a twenty two carat gold setting." Mister Taylor said.

"Then this is not glass or costume jewelry?" Roy asked.

"No! This ring could be worth a lot of money. I would like to get a photo of it and do more research on it." The jeweler said.

Mister Taylor took his photos and gave Roy the box with the ring inside and Roy walked out the door feeling very good about his latest purchase.

Brenda's birthday was coming up soon and Roy wanted to have a little party for her.

Brenda's sister suggested they have it at her house. Brenda and her sister made a big meal with all the trimmings and cake and ice cream. When someone asked about the number of candles on the cake, Brenda lied about her age, again. It seems that lying is something that runs in the family. I may have to help Roy on this score.

Roy had wrapped the ring in some very wild look-ing paper and laid it next to a lamp on a coffee table without any fanfare.

When Brenda was opening the presents, she spot-ted the little box on the coffee table and opened it. She was overwhelmed and pulled it out and put it on her finger for all to see.

In a minute, Cathy's voice can be heard with a snide tone in her voice loud enough for everyone to hear, while Brenda held her hand up for everyone to see the ring.

"Who would give her something like that?" She said pointing at the ring.

Everyone in the room turned to look at Roy and smiled. Cathy's ploy didn't work. Too bad!

Roy waved modestly and smiled.

I have seen this ring and its companion pieces be-fore. The ring is a piece out of a collection of a royal family in Jordan, which is centuries old. It is worth thousands, maybe more, maybe a lot more. Roy kept silent about this little fact, since both of Brenda's girls were sitting there with their vulture look on. He doesn't know the facts as yet. There are more to come.

Later Laurie pointed out that Moms engagement ring isn't big enough. She said this knowing that she would be able to beg mom for money and mom would give her the ring. Then Laurie could pawn it and take the money for herself. Laurie has always stooped to petty things like that.

"I think the ring is just right, dear. But thanks for noticing it." Brenda said.

"What are you going to do now, Mom?" Cathy asked.

"We're going to get married soon and then we're moving to Columbus." Mom said.

"Oh, mommy, please don't go." Laurie said.

Laurie always plays that game. If she can keep mom close to her, she can get more from her. Simple.

This time it didn't work and Laurie and Cathy were on their own for the first time. Good!

The wedding was scheduled for the seventeenth of June. It would take place at the First Methodist Church on Church Street. The minister there said he would be glad to do the wedding and have the reception in his church.

Both of the girls were forced into finally finding a job, a place to live and providing for themselves, maybe even a husband, if they were lucky. I feel sorry for the guy they pick. Something like that has never happened before, for either of them. This little act also frees Roy of two large millstones around his neck.

Neither of them wanted to be in the wedding party, but again, they were forced into it. They don't like to be on the receiving end of being forced, but they both enjoy being on the giving end.

The wedding came off as planned. It was a very small guest list. Roy's parents and three friends and three of Brenda's friends.

During the festivities, Roy's dad got a peek at some paperwork that was left on a table and Dad now knows Brenda's actual age. The papers looked like they had been left by someone accidentally.

Roy and Brenda sped off in a rental car to his dad's house, where they changed clothes and traded the car for the pickup, then on to Roy's house where they hid out for the weekend.

Roy will keep the pickup truck. He will paint it black in Dad's garage, so it's not so easy to see. It seems like bad luck won't leave him alone, but it's not the bad luck, it's Lucy.

It wasn't until after they had been married for a while that Brenda told Roy that she did not want any more kids and he should get a vasectomy. Roy wanted to have children. Not many, one or two, maybe a girl and a boy.

This subject was very, very damaging to their relationship. And ultimately, their marriage, which was doomed to divorce from the start.

Later in the month, someone broke into the house and stole all the jewelry. The police and everyone else had suspicions about who did the robbery, but no proof was found. And none of the pieces were found. But I know where it is. I'll tell Roy when the time is right.

The jewelry store was robbed also, but the crooks didn't find what they were looking for. They took some valuable jewelry, but it will turn up later.

The police came to interview Roy and Brenda about the ring. Roy told them he could give them a description of the ring and the name of the jeweler who took a photo of it. They were overjoyed.

"It is a big ring. It has a full carat diamond in the center, surrounded by a circle of sparkling emeralds, that is surrounded by a circle of emerald cut amethyst, and a circle of small ten point diamonds around the outside, all mounted in gold." Roy said.

"It was Taylor Jewelers where the photos of the ring were taken. I'm sure Mister Taylor will give you one of them and any other information that might help." Roy said.

One of the Police hurried to Taylor Jewelers for more information and a photo.

"There is a necklace of the same design with it. The necklace was designed to wrap around the neck and hang down to the breastplate." Mr. Taylor said. "The whole set is very valuable."

The Officers thanked them and went on their way.

Chapter 26

Brenda Buys A Car

Brenda and Roy had talked about finding Brenda a car to do her errands and drive to work.

Roy looked in the paper and asked around to a few friends, but nothing fell out of the trees.

Then one day a friend of Brenda told her that a friend of hers said that they knew a guy that had an old car for sale cheap. So Brenda went with her friend to see the car.

"Isn't it a beauty?" The guy that was selling the car said.

"Does it run? Can we start it?" She asked.

"You bet. It runs good. There's a little dent in that fender, but that can be pounded out and it'll look as good as new." He said.

What a load.

"But there's a dent in this fender too." She said.

He blew it off.

"Go ahead, start it up. You'll see." He said.

Brenda slid in and turned the key and it started without any hesitation. It didn't smell bad. It didn't look too bad except for the dents. It's white and it cleans up pretty good.

"How much are you asking for it?" She asked.

"One fifty is all." He said.

"Oh! That's tough. I've only got a hundred. Is there a clear title and will you give me a bill of sale so I can get plates?" She asked.

"You bet. I've got a title and I'll give you a bill of sale." He said. "You said you have a hundred on you now?"

"Yes."

"We have a deal." He said and ran to get the title.

He came back soon and had the title but no pad of paper and pen.

"I said I need a bill of sale to get my plates. No bill, no sale." She said.

He hurried back inside and this time came out with pen and paper. The two of them made up the bill of sale and signed and dated it and she handed him the money, and he handed her the title.

Brenda and her friend drove back to Brenda's sister's house. Brenda was excited to show it to Sally.

The next morning Brenda was up early and in a hurry to get to the courthouse and get her plates.

Brenda was at the door of the DMV in the courthouse fifteen minutes before they opened. There were two others ahead of her and that made her mad and infuriated her. How dare they get here before me? She thought.

She finally heard the girl say "next" when it was her turn and he quickly walked to her desk and handed the two pieces of paper to her. The girl addressed her computer and picked up the phone. Within a minute or two there were two uniformed police standing next to Brenda's chair.

"Excuse me ma'am, would you please come with us?" He said.

Brenda took the papers from the girl and followed the police officers.

"Where did you get these papers, ma'am?" The officer asked.

"From the man I bought the car from." Brenda said.

"You bought this car? When was that?' He asked.

"Just yesterday." She said.

"Who sold the car to you?" He said.

"This guy with his name on the bill of sale." She said.

"Did you know that this car is stolen, ma'am?" He asked.

"No!" She seemed shocked.

"Let's go see this man." He said.

The officers and Brenda took a ride to the man's house where she bought the car.

The officers knocked and the man appeared at the door. The officers asked him where he found this car that he sold to this woman.

"I bought the car from Crossroads Chevy." He said.

Now there are four passengers in the Squad car and the next stop is Crossroads Chevy.

The manager of Crossroads Chevy was the first person that the Officers wanted to talk to.

"Wait a minute, I don't sell stolen cars. I got this car from JJ." Mister Nelson said.

"Who and where is JJ?" The officer asked.

Mister Nelson gave directions to JJ's lot to the police officers and they were off back to the courthouse.

The officers gave their report to the Desk Sergeant and Dispatch sent an unmarked car with two detectives to the address given by Mister Nelson.

The detectives phoned in that they had found dozens of stolen cars and arrested all the employees. Would they please send backup and a van to carry all the people to the jail?

Now that Brenda was back with the living, she thought she would have no more surprises coming her way. Surprise!

"We called the original owner of the car you bought from this man. We feel certain that the seller knew it was stolen. This was the reason it was priced so cheaply to you."

"Ah, here is the owner now. Did you bring the original title, sir? He asked.

"Yes I did." Roy said. "I also brought a photo my dad took of me with the car when we first got it." He handed the title and the picture to the police officers. "It has a dent in the right front fender."

"Do you know either of those people in that room, sir?" He asked.

"Why yes, that is my fiancée, but I don't know the man." Roy said.

"She didn't know that this Ford Fairmont was yours?" He asked.

"No. It was stolen before we met." Roy said. "Yes, we were just talking about her finding a car to drive to work, and she called me last night to say that she found a really good car and it was so cheap that she paid for it right then and would get the plates today." Roy said.

The officers decided that Brenda had no part in the stolen car business, and did not arrest her.

"Brenda. Are you alright? How did you get involved with all this?" Roy asked.

Brenda didn't want to talk right now. She wanted her car and plates for it!

One of the police officers walked with her to the DMV and stayed there until the title problem was resolved. Brenda is now the proud owner of a white 1978 Ford Fairmont Wagon with dents in the fenders.

The police had a field day with JJ and his crew. All were arrested and jailed pending court appearances. All of the cars were impounded and the owners were contacted. Some of the local owners showed up immediately, but some were out-of-towners.

Mister Nelson told the police that he would offer to buy any of the cars that were unclaimed or if the owners didn't want to keep them.

Jethro Jones is now out of business.

Chapter 27

Donna

Roy got dragged to this meeting of a bunch of women talking about a business that you work out of your home selling stuff. He decided to sit it out on a couch against the back wall. After only a few minutes, a woman about his age came and sat next to him on the couch.

"Hi. Can I sit with you? This meeting wasn't anything that I thought it would be." She said.

Roy hadn't been looking in her direction until she spoke. Now he was staring at the most beautiful woman he had ever seen before.

"I – uh – I guess. - Wow. - I'm Roy Spencer. - Nice to meet you." He said.

He extended his hand to her and she took it in her hand. She held his hand for a few seconds more than normal and slowly released it with a smile.

"I'm Donna Miles. My girlfriend dragged me to this meeting so she could have someone to ride with." She said.

"Yeah, me too."

He didn't know what he was saying.

"What do you do Roy?" She asked.

"I'm in electronics at the radio station WZNP in Newark." He said. "What about you?"

"I'm a florist. I worked for years in my families business. I grew up in New Castle, Indiana. It is the rose capital of the world. Well, maybe not the world, but the country." She said and that little tinkling giggle surfaced.

"So, can I call you Rosey?" He asked.

She giggled again and said, "No silly. You can call me Flora." And she began to giggle and couldn't stop.

Roy put his hand on her shoulder and she slowly cruised to a stop and smiled at him.

"Could I hold your hand again?" She asked.

"Sure." He laid his hand on the cushion between them and she laid her hand on his.

"You have a gentle feel to your hand. Kind of a feel of peace. Is that the way with your whole body?" She asked.

"I think so. I never gave it much thought. Why do you ask?" He said.

"My husband's hand and body feels so tense all the time, like he was about to explode." She said.

"Will you be coming to these meetings again?" He asked.

"If you will be here, I will too." She said.

"Yes. I will put it on my calendar so I won't forget." He said.

She lit up with a big bright smile that could have been seen all around the room.

"I think we are going to be friends, Roy." She said. She began to giggle that little tinkling sound again, but only for a few seconds, and stopped and composed herself.

The meeting broke up and she jumped up and ran toward the front of the room where all the women were beginning to stand up.

During that week, Roy thought of Donna several times. He remembered how gentle she was. He thought about her concern and sensitivity toward others. He imagined what it would be like to sit and talk with her for days. Her great beauty was not lost in his thoughts, either.

The next Wednesday Roy was seated in the same place and just as he had hoped, the most beautiful girl in the world came into the room and sat beside him. He suddenly began to feel special.

"Hi." She said. "I'm really glad you could make it tonight."

"I am too. I enjoy staring at a beautiful woman. It makes me feel like I'm doing something right." He said.

"Do you think we could go somewhere to be alone for a little while?" She said.

His heart leapt for joy in his chest, but he kept himself calm. It was difficult, but Roy is strong.

"We could go sit in my car, if you want." He said.

"Good! Let's go."

They moved slowly and quietly out the back door and away from the meeting room. It only took another minute to get to Roy's car.

"You said 'your husband' before. Do you have kids too?" He asked.

"Yes, I have two boys, seven and eight." She said.

"I wish I had a couple kids of my own." He said and the smile on his face faded.

There were many things he noticed about her while they sat inside on the couch. She is about five foot seven, thin but not skinny, shoulder length almost red hair that is well taken care of, nice clothes, not flashy. But here in the car, there was one distinct thing he noticed. She had the most wonderful smell about her.

Being a dumb guy, he had no idea what the smell was, but he knew he liked it and he had never come across it before. Ever after that he noticed it every time they met.

During the week, every week, she would pop into his mind and say 'hello'. He enjoyed that but again he said nothing and remained calm.

Roy and Donna met at the weekly meeting every week from then on. They would sneak out the back door and into his or her car every week for as long as the meetings were held there.

They talked about everything that was in the news, the weather, her flowers, his school, boating, baseball, football, business, that new store in the mall, and anything else that might come up. Never politics or religion.

"I forget. You didn't tell me what you do. Did you?" He said.

"Yes. I have a little florist shop down on the square. We have five acres in Vanatta where I grow all the flowers that will grow in this area. I have a lot sent in from other parts of the country too. Of course, all the roses come from New Castle." She said.

"What about you?" She asked.

"I live and work in Newark. I am married to a woman who has two half grown girls and does not want any more kids. But I would like to have at least one of my own. Actually I would like to have a girl and a boy. But it looks like I won't be able to do that." He said. Again the smile faded and his face became sad.

They only wanted to be away from the noise and the people. But mostly they wanted to be together and this was the only way they could see to do it.

"I keep the transmitter for the radio station on the air, and fix all the small stuff like microphones and amplifiers. Here's one of my cards if you ever want to contact me." He said.

"Roy, I've noticed that you have never tried to grab me or even touch me. Are you afraid of me?" She asked.

"No, but you're married and so am I. I wouldn't want to start something that I couldn't finish or get someone in trouble." He said.

"I really appreciate that. You do know that this is the last of these meetings. We won't be sitting in our cars together again. I'm going to miss this." She said.

"So am I." He said. Now he had a good reason for the smile to fade away, and he was sorry about that.

They both hurried in the back door and she stopped as she entered the outside door.

"Wait. I can't let you go without a hug." She said.

She turned around before she opened the inner door and hugged him. He, of course, had wanted to hug her for months, responded willingly to her hug with one of his own.

They stood there for only a few minutes until the feeling of joy subsided. Then she opened the door and slowly moved into their original positions on the couch.

The reason Roy didn't see Donna around town was that she lived in Vanatta. Roy didn't get to Vanatta very often. Maybe he might take a ride up there once in a while.

It was a nice thought, but Brenda had other ideas about where Roy would be driving and where he would be spending his time. The answer was always the same, 'with her'.

Chapter 28

A Hard Life

It's been a hard life for Roy.

He never was a big kid when he was growing up. He was picked on by the older, bigger boys, and sometimes girls too. There was lots of trouble in school from elementary all the way through high school. He did find some friends though, here and there.

The Army was no fun either. He didn't want to be an electronics technician, but he was good at it. He could dope out a problem with an amplifier that he had never seen before. Other guys had given up on it, and Roy fixed it.

He was sent to a cold miserable place and spent nearly two years there. He had to put up with one particularly mean guy who thought he was better than every one else in the world. Since Roy has a good spirit, there were others that recognized it and become his friends.

The mean guy did not have the good spirit and ultimately someone in authority saw how bad he was and sent him away.

He studied at a college for some time, and actually added to his experience and knowledge about his craft. Soon a job came along and even though it was not a high paying job, he stayed with it.

A woman entered his life. Too bad he didn't recognize the faults she had and the meanness she brought with her. Brenda did some nice things for Roy, but most of them were designed to get something from him for her. She stole money from his savings, from his wallet and from anywhere he might have hidden it.

She brought two mean girls who hated Roy before they even met him. Mom was far more important than any man in the world. These two hated each other and any one who might accidentally come between them and Mom.

It seems like bad luck won't leave him alone. But it's not bad luck, it's Lucy.

They tried every trick in the book to get rid of Roy, but none of them worked. They lied, cheated and stole every chance they got. Brenda saw the possibilities of a good life of leisure, and she was not going to let two deceitful girls ruin it for her. .

Both girls told lies about Roy to anyone who would listen, but Brenda knew the truth.

Roy had an old house that was not worth much, but it was his. He was always fixing it. It was a good thing that his dad taught him all he knew about carpentry and masonry.

Roy worked all his life in the radio station and lived in a mediocre house. Those two girl kids didn't like him. He was always scratching for money, but his wife, Brenda, spends it all as fast as she can get it. And what she doesn't spend, she steals and hides in hidden savings accounts.

He had a really old car that barely got itself around. When that was replaced by a car that was way newer, it was stolen. Roy and his dad got a real gift when they found that old Studebaker truck. They went through it from top to bottom and repaired everything. It ran like new, but looked old. A perfect fit for Roy.

Roy married Brenda and the girls saw an opportunity to hitch their wagon to Mom and Roy and not have to work for the rest of their lives. Things change and there sometimes is nothing you can do about it. The girls never saw this coming. After the wedding, Brenda told the girls that she and Roy would be moving out of town and that they were not invited. What a stroke of genius on Roy's part.

Brenda told the girls that they were moving to Columbus for Roy's job. But they didn't. They only did it to get rid of the girls. Roy bought a different house, one two three Harris Street. In a different side of town, called Heath. With a different phone number. But he still works at the radio station in the same job. He even went to the courthouse and changed his name to Spencer Miller.

All in hopes that those girls wouldn't find him. It worked!

Roy and his dad painted the old '58 Studebaker truck black, put on black wall tires and recovered the seat with a nondescript seat cover. It looks totally different, and unless you knew your cars, you wouldn't recognize it.

Roy went into hiding!

Just to make sure, Roy and his dad added a garage to the old house he was living in and hid the truck in it.

When the divorce happened, Brenda said that she wanted the house, but since Roy was smart enough to buy the house himself and have it put in his name only, she had no claim to it. She packed everything in her '78 Ford Fairmont Wagon and drove away.

Much later he found out that all she wanted was money and security, not his kids. They finally got divorced. It took a long time for Roy to even think that she would do such a low life thing to him. But he never knew her.

Roy never did find the money that Brenda put away in the various savings accounts, but what she doesn't know is that it is all about to go away, and she won't even remember any of the details. Too bad!

Roy was still working at the radio station as a DJ and an engineer, and continued to fill those positions. Once the divorce was started he no longer had any contact with either of the girls or with Brenda. Funny how that works.

For many years after the divorce, Roy worked at the radio station doing everything he could to help. He kept his house looking good and he dated a few women, but with no real interest. He was single again, but didn't want another marriage.

Every once in a while, he thought about the pretty girl with the funny giggle, and wished he could find her. But he had no luck there.

Once he goes back in time to do it all over again, the right way, things will change for the better. I picked the right date, the right age and the right place to go to. All he has to do is listen to me and do the right thing.

I told him, "You are not losing it until you stop getting up."

Chapter 29

Nicholas

Roy has had a grueling life and he is about to turn fifty years old, again. I will meet him tomorrow and if he can say the right thing, we can repair most of the terrible things in his life.

I can't explain to you how this will happen. It is enough to say that it will, and I will be required to manage every little thing so Lucy is kept away from him.

We will retreat to the day Roy entered high school in ninth grade. One very good thing is that Roy will have memories to guide him through certain parts of his life. Memories remind us of what is important. After that part is repaired, that memory will disappear. It would be too confusing to explain to you, and besides, I'm not allowed to tell secrets.

We will meet again when he turns fifty years old. I hope I get everything right by then. This is the hardest part of my job.

Cathy and Laurie have given Roy a bad time for all of his life that they knew him, but that is all coming to and end now. Once he speaks the magic words.

"Roy, I'm Nicholas Tanner. I am here to tell you a little story. Let's have a seat, this will be a long story and you might get tired of it."

I told Roy the whole story of his life and he was shocked. He doesn't know what to do now. None of the others knew what to do either until I explained everything to them.

"You must be careful not to talk to, or listen to, Lucy. It is vital to your survival."

"What do you mean, you don't know who Lucy is? The guy in the red pajamas with the horns. He can look like anyone he wants, man or woman. He can also look like any animal as well. Unfortunately, I always see him as he really is. Not a pleasant sight, but I have put up with it for centuries."

"Every time I call him Lucy, he gets mad. If I do it well enough and he gets mad enough, he disappears. Then I have a little time without his interference. Good times!"

"Once you say the magic words, everything falls into place. You already know what they are. You have said them hundreds of times over your lifetime. I know, because I have heard them. Once you have said them, you will return to a time which has been pre-set for you and you will start over."

"Oh God, I wish I had married Donna." Roy said.

And there we are! Those are your magic words. And here we go again.

SHIFT

Chapter 31

Roy Goes To School, Again

Roy was an ordinary kind of a guy, with all the hopes and dreams that everybody has. He wasn't an Adonis, but he wasn't ugly either. I have told this story hundreds of times and no one ever believes it.

I have known Roy for many years. We actually met on the day of his fiftieth birthday, but I have followed him ever since he was born. He is a fascinating person.

Roy had a pretty normal childhood. He was a little clumsy sometimes, but most kids are that way. He was a little slow in school in the early years. He improved a lot as he got older, also pretty normal. But now he was on his way to high school and things were about to change. Again.

He was a C student for most of his time in school. If he worked a little more at it he could become a B student, but Lucy got to him before I did. I'll just whisper to him from time to time until the allotted time.

He was not very athletic. He could throw and catch a ball. And run. Could he run! The one thing that he could do well was run, and fast, very fast!

Roy always liked football, but older kids always told him that he was too small. It's amazing what mean kids will do.

It was the last week of the season and Roy finally had a chance to see a high school football game that night. He was sitting with a friend who played on the team, at the very end of the bench, when the coach motioned to him.

The game was almost over and they had one more chance to score.

"Hey, you! Come here!" He called to Roy. "Run this out to the quarterback, it's our next play!"

Roy took the slip of paper the coach had and ran it to the quarterback and ran back to his seat.

The coach watched him on the way out and back the way coaches do. Coaches always have a stopwatch in their hand. This coach did too, and he absent-mindedly timed Roy's run.

Suddenly the coach had lost interest in the play he sent out.

"That's crazy!" He said. "Hey kid, come here!"

Roy walked to the coach. "Yes sir?" He said.

But now, the game was over and the team was already running off the field.

"Go up to the forty yard line and when I tell you, I want you to run as fast as you can to the end zone." Coach said.

Roy trotted up to the forty and waited for the coach to tell him.

The coach got himself ready and with his stopwatch in hand had Roy run the forty yards to the goal line.

"Four point one?" Coach Miller said out loud.

"I don't believe it!" He said. "That's the fastest time I have ever seen a kid your age run the forty."

"Listen kid, when school starts next year, I want you to come to the field and talk to me. No one else! Just me! OK?" He said. "The first day!"

"Sure coach. On the first day." Roy said.

Roy didn't tell anyone that he was going out for football. So there was no one to laugh at him and make fun of him for wanting it to happen. Lucy lost this time.

He went out for football in his freshman year and made the team as a tight end. The coach knew he could run, but the big surprise was that he could catch the ball too. It didn't matter where the quarterback threw the ball, Roy caught it.

All summer long Roy was involved with the football practices. One guy even kicked the ball over the uprights and Roy ran and caught it. The whole team knew they had something special and there was talk of winning the State.

During the summer, Roy worked out in the weight room nearly every day. By the time football season began Roy had added a lot of muscle and endurance. Now he's five foot nine and one hundred forty pounds. Getting better.

Coach Miller took a special interest in Roy. He knew he had him for the four years remaining in school. Now he had to make him into a superstar.

Roy made the team easily. He would play what the coach called Receiver. If the quarterback couldn't find a tight end or a wide receiver in the play who was supposed to catch the ball, he threw it to Roy. Roy would catch everything and best of all, he would run it in for a touchdown almost every time.

The Newark Panthers had a few bad football years. They had a good quarterback and some good linemen, but no one could catch the ball. Now here comes Roy. He can run faster than anyone on the team and he can catch the ball too.

Newark won the first game by two touchdowns. The school celebrated loudly and long over the weekend. Roy was instantly famous throughout the school.

Suddenly all the girls who wouldn't even look at him were falling all over him. He dated a few girls here and there, but all they wanted was to be seen with the football hero, even if he only drove an old Ford pickup. I had to whisper in his ear several times, "You've got something better waiting for you."

Roy's dad saw a few years ago that Roy would need transportation to and from school and for some of the errands his mother would dream up. Dad found a '62 Ford pickup at one of his friend's house and bought it for him. Dad and Roy worked on it for a couple weeks and got it running good enough for Roy to use.

He was still very self-conscious, although he had no need to be, so he was not very good with girls, but he was good to them, and he was getting better. He finally began to listen to me. He could have had every girl in school if he wanted.

From the time he was young, his dad showed Roy how to use tools. Starting with the hammer and saw, then all the carpentry tools and then all the masonry tools. His dad built the family house with Roy's help.

During the three years it took to build their house, Roy received a Master's Degree in Carpentry and

Masonry from Dad U. He learned how to frame up walls of a house and build a post and beam building. He understood the names and uses of everything from a jig saw to a block plane.

He learned how to set forms, pour concrete, screed the mud and float finish it. He could mix mortar and lay bricks and concrete blocks too. He understood the names and uses of everything from a trowel to a bull float. But Roy didn't want to be a carpenter or a brick layer as a profession.

Roy could build a whole house by himself if he had the materials. He was not too good with plumbing, but electricity was easy for him.

Roy wanted to do something that he could help other people. He didn't know what that was, but he was sure it wasn't carpentry or masonry or any of the things that had to do with building houses.

His parents helped him as much as they could with books, encyclopedias, tapes and anything that they thought would help him with his schoolwork.

But in the mean time he was playing football for Newark High School and loving it.

When the second game began, the Panthers were to receive the ball in the first quarter. The kick off went straight to Roy. He caught it and ran it back ninety five yards for a touchdown.

The Panthers rejoiced and they kicked off to the opposing team. After the second down, Coach Miller sent Roy in to play Safety. The quarterback for the other team dropped back after the snap and threw a long one to his wide receiver. There was only one problem. Roy was where the ball came down and not their receiver. Roy caught it and took it to the house. Score Panthers 14, Visitors 0.

It went that way for the rest of the game and the Panthers won another game.

Roy continued to play in what the coaches thought was an amazing way. It was just Roy, doing what comes naturally.

The rest of the games that year went in much the same fashion. Roy would get the ball and take it in for a touchdown. Over and over all year long.

The Panthers went to the State tournament and won the first two games easily, but the championship game was a whole different thing. The opponents overwhelmed the offensive line and sacked the quarterback four times. Roy was open downfield, waving his arms, at each of those times. Two of which resulted in fumbles and the opponents scoring a touchdown.

Even with all that Roy could do, nothing could keep them from losing the game.

Now that the football season was over, Roy got serious with his studies. He knew he had something to accomplish some day and he wanted to be ready.

The sophomore year was going to be a big one for Roy and the Panthers. Roy had a growth spurt over the summer and added three inches to his height. Now six foot tall Roy would have looked more ominous had he been in the quarterback position. Coach Miller found two big juniors who said they would play at the Guard and Tackle positions. This could be what they needed to finally win the State.

Roy thought the classes he had this year were easy, but in truth, they were things he had studied, but didn't sink in very well before. He maintained a B minus average for the year, but there were a couple of Cs.

Football season started the same as every year, lots of studying, lots of time for practice and even more time working out in the weight room.

Roy put on nine pounds over the winter. That doesn't sound like very much, but with a fifteen year old kid, it's a lot. Especially when it's all muscle.

The Panthers season went well for five games and they were at five and oh. Roy got hurt in the fifth game and had to sit out the sixth. They lost the sixth by one touchdown. Coach Miller and the other coaches soon realized the complete value of having Roy on the field.

Roy was back in business in the seventh game and they won again. The State championship was in view. The whole team bore down and won the rest of the games that season.

The State tournament went very well with the Panthers winning the first two and now entering the championship game. Their opponent was the same team that beat them so badly last year. But Coach Miller had a new plan. Roy became a decoy. The other team doubled and triple teamed him to the point that all the other players were open many more times than before. The Panthers ran all over their opponent and won the State.

Newark went crazy! Everyone celebrated for days. The weekend was one long party. Roy was approaching superstar status, and Coach Miller was loving it.

So far, Roy has filled up his brain with math and English, algebra and composition, science and biology, history and several electives like Spanish. And football, lots of football.

Even though Roy doesn't play all the positions on the field, he thought he should know what each of them did and how they did it. One of the main positions Roy was trying to learn was the field general, the quarterback.

Roy would practice with a football at home, but he just couldn't master the grip and the throw. If he held it right, he couldn't throw it. If he could throw it, it wouldn't go where he wanted it. It took him a while, but he finally decided that the quarterback position was not for him. Good choice.

Roy's junior year started like the last two. Football practices, new classes new kids, new players, but the same old grind.

Football practice took on a new look since the quarterback was a senior and he was gone now. Coach Miller had three guys who were trying out for the job. He told Roy to get on the fifty yard line and catch anything he could from these three guys.

The coach had someone bring a big bag of balls and hand them to the three guys. Then they were to throw them to Roy, who would try to catch them. It was a huge success and very funny to watch.

The first guy threw the ball several times and it would only go to the forty yard line. The next guy threw it and it went almost to the sideline. The third guy threw it and it went very high but only ten or twelve yards in front of him.

Roy, of course, caught all three of them.

The coach was shaking his head and wringing his hands.

"What do you think? Roy?" Coach asked.

"We can't use these guys. Hey wait! Look! Here comes someone!" He said pointing across the field.

"Hey Coach, could I try out for the football team?" He asked.

"Sure. What's your name? What do you do?" Coach asked.

"Sam O'Neill, sir. I can throw the ball, but I can't catch it very good. Is that OK?" He said.

"Come on over here. Now you stand right here and throw the ball to that guy out there." Coach said.

Roy was at the twenty yard line.

The kid threw it to him. Right to him.

Coach motioned to Roy to move farther back. Roy moved to the thirty, then the forty, then the fifty. Each time he threw it right to Roy. They tried running plays up and down the field, across the field and circle routes. He performed better than they expected.

"I think we have a new quarterback." Coach said.

It turned out that there would be several new players on the Panthers team. A couple of new linemen will help keep out unwanted opposing players trying to get to the quarterback.

Football practice was looking like it would be fun this season. And it was. The Panthers worked very hard for all of the month of August and into

September. Practice games, pre-season games and then the real thing.

The linemen stopped the intruders, Sam threw the ball to Roy and Roy ran it in for a touchdown. Once they got it down pat, it seemed pretty simple. The Panthers had rehearsed this act over and over. When it was time for the big day they performed beautifully.

Roy studied plane geometry, U. S. History, and several others along with football. It was nice that he was finally bringing home B's and the occasional A. And an occasional girlfriend.

The Panthers were unstoppable this season. They rolled over everyone and continued up to and including the State championship. This was the second time Roy was on the winning team. He was becoming a star.

Over the summer, there were girls forcing themselves on him at least once a week during the vacation. He got quite a lesson in how girls act and think. I had to keep reminding him what he really wanted. Fortunately, Roy listened to me this year. There are several important things he needs to do.

I gave him several hints about girls and what to look for. He has listened to all of my suggestions and paid attention to most of them. Occasionally he stops thinking and listening and just charges forward. I told him that would get him into trouble, but he has to learn.

Roy is a senior now, a big star football player and the winner of two State championships in a row.

What more could any one want. Well Roy wanted to be out of high school.

He knew what was coming this year. The whole school would be expecting Roy to lead the football team to another State championship. There had not been a school to win three in a row since the nineteen twenties.

All of the hardest classes were saved for the seniors. He has had plane and solid geometry, but now there's trigonometry and physics and social studies. And football.

By now football had become almost automatic with Roy. He didn't need to practice. He just stood out there on the field and they threw to ball to him.

This season went much like the others. The other players were a lot better and the new linemen were big and strong. Roy had put on a few more pounds of muscle and an inch in height. He was pretty hard to miss on the field.

The new quarterback could throw the ball through a tire hanging on a tree limb at thirty yards. And Roy could catch it. The Panthers had an unbeaten season. If Newark had been a person, it would have been jumping up and down.

They rolled into the playoffs and took the State championship by three touchdowns. Roy was named the Most Valuable Player for the second time.

But what he was thinking was, "What now?"

The answer to that came very soon. He studied and took his finals and graduated.

He had worked his tail off to get here. There were so many negatives working against him, he wasn't sure he could do it. But he did!

There was a man sitting in his seat in the auditorium. It was me and I stood up and told him, "Sit right here Roy." He sat and he was alone.

The next thing Roy heard was his name being called in the graduation ceremony.

"Charles Roy Spencer."

Roy stood and walked along the prescribed route until he met Mr. Winters standing in the middle of the stage. He took Mr. Winters' outstretched hand with his right hand and received the cardboard tube with his left.

"Congratulations Roy."

When Mr. Winters released his hand, he spoke his name again and Roy made his way back to his seat. He reached up and moved the tassel to the left side of his cap. He was a High School graduate! His return to his seat was a blur, but he made it. He graduated!

He was eighteen and the future looked bright. He had many choices, college, the military, or something else.

Chapter 32

Roy Goes To College, Again

It was the week before the end of school and many college and business representatives were in the auditorium to talk the students into coming to their school.

Roy had talked to every college representative who came to the school, and listened intently to all their sales pitches, but none of them made him feel good about what he wanted to do with his life. He wanted to help people, but none of these offered anything like that.

Way at the back of the auditorium, was one man sitting at a small table with two small signs, telling about his school.

"Hi." Roy said. "What is this about?"

The man perked up. This was the first student to even look at his table.

"I'm from the Midwest Chiropractic College. We are located here in Newark a block off the square. What can I help you with?" He asked.

"What does a chiropractic do?" Roy asked.

"Not a chiropractic, a Chiropractor." He said.

"The Chiropractor works on the restoration of a normal function of the nervous system. The nervous system controls all the other functions of the body. A normal nervous system protects the body and restores it to normal." He said.

"Chiropractors do not prescribe medicine or practice surgery." He said.

Roy and the man from the school sat and talked for the rest of the time until the high school began to turn off the lights and close the doors.

"Would you like to come with me and look into the school?" He asked.

"Yes, I would!" Roy said. This might be the one, thought Roy. This might just be the one!

"Would you like to follow me? What are you driving?" He asked.

"I have that little red Datsun pickup." Roy said as he pointed at it. It was a few years old with a few dents and a lot of miles on it, but it ran good, worked hard and got good mileage. And it still looked good.

It didn't take long for Roy to know that this was the right thing to do. He signed up right then to attend the school and become a Chiropractor.

Roy was thinking about going to Med School and becoming a doctor, but a long time ago, he found that the sight of blood made him sick. That stopped the medical part of his plan.

"You will need two years of undergraduate classes in Pre-Med school to qualify and apply to MCC." He said.

"What is your name?" He asked.

"Roy Spencer."

"Oh, you're the big football star here. You were named MVP, weren't you?" He said.

"Yes, sir."

"I heard that you received a full scholarship at Ohio State." He said.

"Yes, but they don't have what I want." Roy said.

"You could go for two years in the Pre-Med Course there and then transfer to The Chiropractic College here in Newark. We would be glad to have you. We can't offer you a scholarship, though." He said.

Boy, that solved a big problem for Roy. He began to smile again.

"We will have a seat with your name on it once you finish the Pre-Med Course at Ohio State." He said.

Roy was feeling much better now that he talked to the recruiter from the college. He was going to work harder than he ever had to become a Doctor of Chiropractic (D.C.)

Roy was offered a football scholarship to Ohio State, but they did not have a course where he could learn to be a Chiropractor. He thought he would be glad to take the Pre-Med course so he could go on to the Chiropractic College.

Roy decided that he had better go to Columbus and talk to the Administrators in case there were any questions.

He drove to the thirty miles Columbus to talk to the Administrators in person. He asked the most important question for his future.

"Will I be able to take the Pre-Med course and then go to the Chiropractic School?" He asked.

They asked their most important question to them.

"Will you play football here for those two years?"

"Yes, of course. I like playing football. I especially like winning. I would like to play for the two years and win everything possible." Roy said.

"In that case we will agree to your proposal." They gave him the name and phone number of the coach, and all the information about the football program. They told him what date, time and the name of the coach he was to meet for the first practice.

Roy drove back home with a huge smile on his face. His parents didn't know what it was all about. Roy explained what he had done and they were ecstatic. There was an air of surprise, joy, hopefulness and rejoicing in their home for many days.

Now Roy wanted to do something that would help keep him in shape and help someone. He went to the Salvation Army and asked them. Nothing there for him, but as he was leaving, a woman told him about the houses being built in town by Habitat.

Habitat was glad to see him. He knew as much as any of the contractors working on the project, and he brought his own tools. He dove in head first.

Roy had spent four years getting his body in shape to play football. All the girls knew what he looked like on the field with all the pads and protection he was wearing, but only a very few knew what he looked like without his shirt on.

Now Roy spent all day, every day working on the Habitat houses with his shirt off and sweating a lot and feeling good about it.

Word got around that Roy was working with Habitat and the girls were lined up at the fences trying to get a good look. Some even had binoculars with them.

He dated one once in a while, but not one made him feel as good as Donna did in his memory. He prayed, he wished, that he could meet this girl in his memory that had him so mystified.

By the time that it was time for Roy to start school in Columbus, he was really ready for football. He had put on weight and muscle and he was as fast as he always was. Ohio State didn't know what they had.

Roy found his notes and reported to the Coach just as the Coach said he should.

"Good morning, Coach. I'm Roy Spencer. I was told to report to you here this morning."

"Yes that's right. I have followed your exploits on the field in Newark. You're good. Can you still do it?"

"I hope so. But I probably need some practice." Roy said.

Coach Hatch called all the players to come to him.

"I'm glad I have you all here. These are the receivers and that one is the quarterback." He pointed to each one.

"OK. Receivers get ready to run and catch the ball. Paul will throw it to each of you. Let's see what we have this year." He said.

Roy was second in line and when the ball was thrown he really had to run to get it, but he did. Each of the other receivers caught the ball.

Next the ball was thrown farther out and one of them didn't quite get to it, but Roy did.

"OK. Now you center it, Eric, and you run a post pattern, Roy, and you throw it, Paul."

They all got into position and Paul threw it and Roy ran as fast as he could and just barely made it for the catch. He finished the run into the end zone with a big smile.

"Very impressive Roy. We don't usually see a freshman with that much ability." Coach said.

Regular practice started the next day. The team worked very hard and the coach could see the team begin to gel.

"OK, you guys. We're not playing high school ball anymore. We're playing teams like Michigan, Northwestern, Michigan State and Penn State. This is not a walk in the park any more. This is the tough stuff." Coach Hatch said.

During the first game the opponents got the kick-off and went three and out. Roy was spotted on the goal line as the return man. Roy caught the punt and ran it back seventy yards to the opponents fifteen. The next play, Paul threw it to one of the wide receivers for a touchdown.

Several plays later, the ball came in Roy's direction, he caught it and ran it in for a touchdown which put Ohio State ahead. The team held on for a win. They all heralded Roy, but the coach told them they were lucky. "Much more strength and concentration is needed." He said.

Practices were harder and more intense for the rest of the month. They lost a big one to Michigan State, but won the others, which made them four and one, and in first place.

The Buckeyes became stronger as the season wore on and they finished in first place, but they did not get an invitation to the Rose Bowl. This was what Coach Hatch and Roy were both hoping for.

They received an invitation to the Cotton Bowl. It was a big deal, but in the eyes of Coach Hatch and Roy, it was a loss. The team vowed to do better next year. The Buckeyes won the game at the Cotton Bowl, but there was still a lot of work to be done. Happy New Year!

Roy realized that he had several months left in school and Pre-Med was not the easiest course in the school. It took work. Lots of work!

From the first day back from vacation, Roy studied day and night to catch up on the Pre-Med courses. It was all foreign to him and it took more than a little work to keep up with the rest of the class.

He had biology, anatomy, chemistry, nutrition and physics. And that was only this semester. He could look for more biology, genetics, biochemistry, human physiology, toxicology, immunology and a lot more in the coming semesters.

He had to finish ninety semester hours of Pre-Med in order to qualify for the Chiropractic College. He knew this and was keeping count of it all at home on a chart on his wall.

Roy put his nose to the grindstone and finished the semester with a B. A much-needed B, I might add. But now it was time to be off for the summer.

Roy knew he must find a job to keep him going through school. The scholarship paid for the school, but there were little things like rent and groceries to think about.

Habitat only built a few houses in town last year and it wasn't a paying job. Roy needed a paying job to save up for food over the school year. Even though he was still living with his parents, he didn't think he should put that much of a big burden on them.

He began a trek through the various construction companies in and out of town. At the third one, the man in charge recognized him and hired him on the spot.

"You worked on the Habitat houses last year didn't you?" He asked.

"Yes sir. It was something I could do to help." Roy said.

"I know one of the foremen there and he was very happy with your work. What are you looking for now?" He asked.

Roy explained why he needed a job and the foreman hired him.

"If you need anything, call me at this number." He said as he handed him his card. It said Palmer Construction, Thomas Palmer and the phone number.

Roy put it into his wallet. He knew he would need it. Roy would start tomorrow and work every day till school started.

"I don't work on Sunday." Roy said.

"No problem. I don't either." The foreman said.

Roy started a savings account just for this money. He put every cent away for the school year. He was paid more money than he expected and it built up in the account pretty fast. He liked that.

Construction is hard work! Even the best jobs and the most menial of jobs are hard. Everyone is tired of being worn out at the end of the day. It took Roy some time to get himself limber and strong enough to do the work. But as always he gave all he had every day. Working construction kept Roy strong all summer long and ready to play football.

One day a man come over to him and asked if he could do a little job at his house for him.

"I would be glad to help if you need it. What is it that you need done?" Roy said.

"I have moved into my mothers house now that she is gone and I would like to exchange that heavy old cast iron sink in the kitchen for a smaller, lighter one. Do you think it would be something you could do?" He asked.

"Sure. Do you have the parts? When would you like to do it?" He asked.

"Yes, everything is on hand. Would Saturday be okay if you're not working here." He said.

"Saturday's good. I'll be there at nine. See you then." Roy said.

Roy was surprised when the man was ready at nine, that's usually too early for the customer. They removed the heavy cast iron sink and Roy did a few presses as he carried it out to his truck. The new countertop went in easily and after careful measurement and even more careful cutting, the new sink was fitted into the special hole.

Roy finished up the plumbing job and the man handed him five twenty dollar bills.

"Thank you, sir. I really appreciate this." Roy said.

"You saved my life with this job. I don't know what I would have done if you hadn't finished this for me." He said. "You have made a friend."

Roy had finished the job before noon and he made a hundred dollars. Wow, what a lucky break.

These kinds of things happened to Roy, what seemed like, every day during the summer. Put this wall up, tear this wall down, build me a porch, build me a deck, build me a fence, build me a brick wall.

In June and July he would do a little side job about once a week. He never asked for money, he just took what they gave him. Each time it was more than he would have charged them, but he took it and put it all in savings.

Most of the jobs were small and easy for Roy, but sometimes the demands were too much for him and he would need someone to help. Then he would have to ask for money to pay someone. The people didn't mind paying, because Roy did excellent work, and everyone knew it.

Late in July, when he had only a few weeks left before football season was to begin, a man came to Roy and asked if he could build a big deck for him.

Roy went with him to his house to inspect the job site and examine the drawings. The man had drawn up a huge multi-level deck stretching across the rear of the house and out into the back yard.

The drawings showed a grilling area with a big stainless steel, five burner grill and a sink. There was a lounging space with couches and chaises under a pergola. And an eating space with a table for eight with rattan chairs and table under a square roof covered with shingles.

"This is going to be very expensive. I will need help and you will probably spend a couple thousand dollars on the materials." Roy told him.

"I have two guys who promised to help. I will buy all the material and have it delivered." He said.

"If the weather holds up, I could have it done in five weeks. I'd like to have half down on a job this big, if you don't mind." Roy said.

"Certainly." The man wrote him out a check for two thousand dollars.

"Wow!" That was way more than Roy thought the whole job was worth, but he took the check.

Roy and the two guys worked day and night for two weeks on the project. They commented on their lack of sleep. They brought in a Bobcat for the dirt work and the two guys did all the concrete work. Once the framing was done plumbers and electricians came to finish their parts. Flooring, benches, posts and walls were soon looming into the night with lights everywhere.

The square shingled roof made the whole place look finished, but a little unusual. Kind of like a cross between a pergola and a gazebo.

The huge job was finished just in time for Roy to start football practice.

As they were walking to their trucks to go home, one of the two men said, "Do you know who that was we did that job for, Roy?"

"No, I never saw him before." Roy said.

"That was the Mayor. You might just be in line for something good." He said.

Roy had put away over five thousand in extra money in his account. Groceries would be a lot easier to buy this winter.

And now it's time to go back to school and football in Columbus.

Roy was getting everything ready for school when a young man stopped by his house. "Is that your little red pickup there?" He asked.

"Yes, why do you ask?"

"I need a pickup and I don't have the money to buy one from the dealers around town. I would like to trade my car for a pickup if I can find someone who will do it." He said.

"What are you driving?" Roy asked."

He pointed across the street. "That Mustang there."

A Mustang! This guy wanted to trade his Mustang for Roy's little pickup? It was a two door hardtop coupe painted yellow that shined like the sun. Yellow!

"By the way, I'm Jim Brown. Not that Jim Brown. He's a lot bigger and richer than I am." Jim laughed.

"I would love the Mustang, but are you sure?" Roy said.

"Yes, I have a house that needs a lot of work and I can't haul anything in my car." Jim said. "Can you tell me about the truck?"

"Sure. It is a few years old but it is in perfect condition. My dad and I have been doing regular maintenance on it. Good tires and it gets thirty miles per gallon. What a bonus." Roy said.

"OK, let's go to the courthouse and do the deal. Could I drive it there to get a feel for it?" Jim said.

"Sure. I'll drive your car then." Roy said.

The trade didn't take long and it didn't cost much either. Now Roy was the proud owner of a shiny little yellow Mustang . Roy was beside himself!

As soon as Roy arrived at the stadium, he saw the coach and some of the players on the field. They had started early. Coach Hatch got a taste of fame from the Big Cotton Bowl. And he wants more.

Once he saw Roy, he called all the players inside and began to talk about winning.

"We don't want to just win. We want to win big! Bigger!" He said.

"If we can beat a team 21 to 14 then we should beat them 41 to 14. That's winning big. We can't get to the Rose Bowl unless we are thought of as the best team in the country. This year, all we will talk about, all we will think about is winning the Rose Bowl." He said.

"I want you to think of yourself as a champion! We are champions! When we win the first game, we will strive to win the second game by a bigger spread! Each time we will win by more! We will be the champions of this division! That is all!" Coach Hatch said and walked out.

Every once in a while when Coach Hatch is on one of his promotional speeches, Roy drifts off to his own life. He knows these last two semesters will be the hardest, and he must get a three point oh average. That's a 'B'! No messing around! And Coach Hatch thinks he has a problem!

Next semester he would have even more difficult courses. Coming up there is Molecular Biology, Organic Chemistry and Kinesiology. Biology was beginning to get under his skin. But one thing about Roy, he plows through it, no matter how hard it is for him. And football.

Football practice this year started like every year before had. Run the patterns, catch the ball, do the tires, hit the blocking dummy, and play practice games.

The team continued to get better and better each day. The first game of the season was coming up soon and Coach Hatch was obsessed with the team being ready.

The Buckeyes won the first game by two touchdowns. Coach Hatch wasn't jumping for joy, but it was a start.

More practices, harder practices, another win. The team continued to win and as Coach Hatch had said, each one was bigger than the last.

The team won every game during the season and ended in first place in the division, again. But this time, all the sports writers were lauding the accomplishments of the team on the coach because of the huge spread of some of the wins.

You could hear Coach Hatch talking to himself about the Rose Bowl. "We are going to the Rose Bowl! I just know it! Why haven't we heard yet?"

Sure enough, the invitation came through and the Buckeyes were invited to the Rose Bowl Game. The coach was elated. He was beside himself with joy. He knew the team would win the big game.

The coach had scheduled their time so that they had six days to practice and get ready for the biggest game in their career.

None of the players had ever been to Pasadena, or for that matter California. The players wanted to see where the parade was held and all the little things that none of them knew anything about.

One of them found a girl who agreed to answer all the questions and show them around.

Paul was named MVP of the game. He threw four touchdown passes. Three of them to Roy. But Paul deserved it. He guided the team through a long hard game and won.

Roy celebrated more than anyone else. No more football practices. Evenings to study his Pre-Med courses. What more could he ask?

All he had to do was finish biology and the rest of his courses with A's and B's.

It was a long school year for Roy. He worked and studied harder this year than ever before. He even received "As" in three of his classes, the rest were graded B. But he was very happy about that. He knew now that he would graduate from the Pre-Med Course and he could move on to the school in Newark.

At the end of the school year it was time for Roy to attend the graduation ceremony and get that valuable diploma.

I was in his seat waiting for him. "Hello, Roy. Would you like to sit here?" When he sat down, I got up and left him alone. I will have a better view from the special place where I will be.

"Charles Roy Spencer."

Roy stood and walked along the prescribed route until he met Mr. Edwards standing in the middle of the stage. He took Mr. Edwards' outstretched hand with his right hand and received the cardboard tube with his left.

"Congratulations Roy."

When Mr. Edwards released his hand, he spoke his name again and Roy made his way back to his seat. He reached up and moved the tassel to the left side of his cap. He was a College graduate! His return to his seat was a blur, but he made it. He graduated!

He was 21 and the future looked bright. Now he was off to Chiropractic College.

Chapter 33

Donna

I don't usually talk to my clients like this, but this was important.

My voice came into Roy's ear. "You need to be in the main hallway of New Castle High School in New Castle, Indiana on Tuesday at two o'clock. That gives you three days. Be dressed properly and cleaned up, this is your only chance."

Roy had to drive all the way from Newark to New Castle, Indiana in order to find the jewel he was wishing for all his life. He parked in front of the high school at two o'clock.

She was standing in the hall reading a notice on the bulletin board when Roy walked up to her. The girl is eighteen and a graduate of this high school.

She was about five foot seven and ninety-nine pounds. She is small proportioned but does not look skinny or frail. She actually looks strong. She is smiling as she is reading the notices.

"Hi. I'm Roy Spencer."

"Hi. I'm Donna Clark." She said as she turned to look at him.

"Do you go to school here?" He asked.

"No, I graduated last year. I'm just here to meet my girlfriend. She's an Associate Teacher." She said, she was still reading the notices.

"Well I came to tell you that I'm in love with you, and I want to marry you." He said.

She quickly turned to look at him again and smiled.

"I don't usually hear a boy tell me he wants to marry me before we've dated." She said with a smile.

"I – uh – I guess I got a little ahead of myself. I want to hold you and kiss you and love you until I die." He said.

Roy was busy stumbling over his tongue. I should have told him what to say. I didn't know he would get crazy at the last minute.

She was intrigued. "Maybe we should just start with the holding part."

He took her in his arms and hugged her. This was the one. He remembered what she felt like when he hugged her and especially how she smelled. It was the same smell and the same feel.

He came back from his thoughts and released her from the hug.

"That was nice. Maybe we can move on to the next step, but not here in the school hallway." She said.

"Would you like to have a hamburger?" He asked.

"Sure."

She directed him to take her to a nice little café across town from the school. They both ordered a hamburger and fries and a Pepsi. He offered to hold her hand and she allowed it.

"You may kiss me now." She said after finishing her hamburger.

He got down on his knees beside the booth and pulled her to him and kissed her. The kiss lasted for several minutes and when he let her go, she said. "Let's try that again."

He took the opportunity to really make an impression with this kiss.

"That's nice. You passed the test and now you go to the next level." She said.

"What test?"

"You didn't grab me when you kissed me." She said.

"What's the next level?"

"I don't know yet, but I'll figure out something." She giggled a tinkling little sound and he remembered that sound, too.

"You said that you wanted to love me. Does that mean you want me to love you physically?" She asked.

"I'd like you to love me with your heart and mind first. Of course I want to make love to you. You are the most beautiful girl – uh – woman I have ever seen. But I hope you will come around to it in your own time." He said.

"Aren't you a little older than I am?"

"Yes, I'm twenty two, and I am going to college and I will soon be working at a job. Is that a problem?" He asked.

He held back because he didn't want her to like him because he was a doctor. He wanted her undivided full attention.

"No. Not at all. It's nice to know that a man like you would show an interest in a skinny young teenager like me." She paused for a moment. "Would you like to go to a movie?" She asked.

He was shocked. She just asked him to a movie with her.

"Sure." What else could he say?

They both enjoyed the movie with many hugs and kisses. He took her home after the movie and asked her if he could see her again.

"I'd like that Roy. You're fun to be with. What did you have in mind?" She asked.

"Nothing really, I just want to be with you. I'll wait for you wherever you say." He said.

"There's a little coffee shop about a block down from the school. Let's meet there. OK?" She said.

"Sounds good to me. What should I order for you?" Roy said.

"I don't know, something different every day." There's that tinkling laugh again.

It was a long drive to New Castle each morning, but Roy knew why he was doing it now.

Roy waited at the coffee shop for ten or fifteen minutes till she came. They had fancy coffee and a cheeseburger, with lots of lettuce and tomato and fries.

"Would you like to see my roses?" She asked.

"I want to see anything you want to show me." Roy said with a lot of enthusiasm.

She started to giggle again at his comment. He reached over and put his hand on hers and she stopped giggling, and smiled at him.

Roy drove and Donna played navigator. She deliberately took the longest way around town to get to the farm.

"Turn here. OK, now left here. Two blocks down stop at the light and turn right." And she would giggle each time. Fortunately Roy recognized the giggle from before and realized that she was having a lot of fun with him. But this fun was not malicious.

It took her nearly an hour for them to go the thirteen blocks from the coffee shop to the farm, but they both enjoyed it since they were together. And laughing.

"Wow! I didn't think it would be this big." He said.

Donna hurried him to the house where her mom and dad were enjoying some applesauce and toast.

"Mom and Dad, this is Roy Spencer. Roy, this is Alice and Daniel Clark, my mom and dad." She said.

I don't usually hear much from my clients, but this one was different.

Donna said very quietly to her Dad. "What do you think Dad?"

"I'll let you know, honey." Dad said.

After the introductions, Roy sat at the table and they gave him some of the applesauce and Mom made him some toast.

"What do you do, Roy?" Dad asked.

"I'm going to school right now. I finished my Pre-Med and now I am going into my second year at the Chiropractic College in Newark."

Boy was dad impressed. I could tell by the expression on his face. A doctor! Wow! Of course Dad said none of that, but he thought it loud and clear.

Donna was surprised. She had only heard Roy tell her he wanted to marry her and other small talk.

They hadn't even hugged and kissed enough to make her sweat.

"Are you going to marry Donna?" Dad asked.

Donna butted in. "Da-a-a-ad!"

"Yes! I asked her that very question just a few days ago. I have not received an answer as yet." Roy said.

"What are you waiting for, dear?" Dad asked.

"He hasn't even touched me yet. I'll let you know!" She said.

"Don't we have somewhere to go Roy?" She said as she bounced up from her chair and shot out the door.

Mom started to say something, but Donna was out the door in a flash.

"Now you see why I don't want to live close to my parents." She said.

"Maybe you could open a florist shop in Newark. I know someone who lives there who would be willing to share a place to live with you." Roy said. He smiled a lot after his invitation.

"You know, that might be a great idea. Actually both of them." She said.

"You could run it. Your parents could supply the flowers until you had a garden full of them at the house. I still have three weeks before school starts again.

They sat in the Mustang for a long time talking and Roy heaved a sigh of relief after she said that she would consider his invitation. He got the car started and headed for Newark and home. It was a long drive and they talked about his and her dreams and what they might be doing to make them come true.

He finally pulled into his driveway and they slowly went into the house and collapsed on the couch.

"You may touch me now." She said.

"Where would you like - - - -?"

She took his hand and carefully placed it exactly where she wanted it. Roy responded slowly and gently to her demands. They sat there with her hand covering his for more than ten minutes.

"Yes, I'll marry you! When would you like to do this huge decision?" She said.

"Would today be too soon?" He asked.

She began to giggle and it took her more than ten minutes for her to slow down and another ten to get herself under control.

"You are so funny! But I understand. I will work on all our plans as quickly as I can. You will be the first to know everything. I promise." And she began to giggle again.

"We have so many items on our 'to do' list, I don't know where to start. Where should I put sex on our list of things to do?" She said and giggled even harder and louder.

"Wherever you want my darling!" Roy said.

"Well, then. You may make love to me now." She said.

"I may?" He said. "Gee, I am so fortunate! But you didn't say 'Please'." He said with a huge smile washing over his face.

"Are you going to make me beg?" She asked.

"What a wonderful idea. The most beautiful woman in the world, begging me, a lowly bum, to make love to her. I don't know if I can handle all this pressure." Roy said. By this time, he was on the couch laughing and rolling around.

She launched herself on top of him and began to beat him with her open hands, while they both laughed and yelled.

"I give up! You win! I will do anything you say." He said.

After Donna's night of fun, there was work to do.

The next big step for them was to find and rent or buy a store front to install the Florist Shop into. Both of them knew this would be the hardest part of the plan.

Roy and Donna sat down and tried to figure out what they could afford to get the flower shop going.

Donna had a small pile of money tucked away in her room at home, but that was in Indiana. With the money was a list of the flowers she wanted to sell and various vendors who handled them.

"I have some money in an account, but it's for groceries during the school year." Roy said.

"We'd better not touch that. Things could get bad if we're not careful." Donna said.

One day Roy was walking into a café, but I stopped him and told him to walk down the block and go into the pawn shop. When Roy looked down into one of the showcases he saw the most beautiful ring he had ever seen.

"Could I see that ring please?" He said.

"A beauty isn't it?' The storeowner said.

"Yes. How much is it?"

"The store owner quoted him a price that seemed very low, and he had enough money in his pocket to buy it. So he did right then.

The storeowner put the ring in a nice box and a little bag and Roy hurried down the street to a fancy jewelry store two blocks away.

Roy walked quickly to Taylor Jewelry and hurried into the store. He showed the ring to the jeweler who looked shocked when he saw it.

"Where did you find this?" He asked.

"In a pawn shop." Roy said.

It is a big ring. It has a full carat diamond in the center, surrounded by a circle of sparkling emeralds, which is surrounded by a circle of emerald cut amethyst, and a circle of small ten point diamonds around the outside, all mounted in gold.

"This is some very fine work and the jewels here are special, this is a twenty two carat gold setting. This ring could be worth a lot of money. I would like to get a photo of it and do more research on it." The jeweler said.

Mister Taylor took his photos and gave Roy the box with the ring inside and Roy walked out the door feeling very good about his latest purchase.

Roy's plan was to put the ring in a safe deposit box in the bank until he could have a real safe at home.

`Roy and Donna were out shopping and Roy stopped and looked at a certain woman.

Roy walked up to her and said. "You look familiar. Who are you?" Roy asked.

"I am Brenda Thomas. Do I know you? Wait I
think I do. You're the football player that won the
State Championship, aren't you?" She asked.

"Yes I did. You have two daughters don't you?"
Roy asked.

"Why, yes, I do." She said.

"How do you know that?" Donna asked.

"Oh I've seen them in school." Roy said.

After they parted ways, Donna said. "Do you
know her?"

"No, I just heard the name." Roy said.

Roy has memories to guide him, but after each
thing is fixed, that memory will go away, and now,
that one is gone.

Chapter 34

Blossoms

Roy has spent much time talking to business people around town about who might have a little building or shop that he could use for the flowers. He has had little or no response so far. Then a man approached him in the grocery store. And we haven't heard much from Lucy lately.

"You're Roy Spencer, aren't you?" He said.

"Yes, I am. What can I do for you? Roy said.

"I think I might have a building for you and your wife." He said.

It seems James Hamilton and a lot more folks in town didn't know that Roy and Donna were not married and Roy was not going to say anything about it right now.

"Wonderful! That would make my day! Who are you and where's this building?" Roy asked.

"I'm sorry, I should have introduced myself. I am James Hamilton, and I own the Newark Advocate. It's the local newspaper. The shop is on the square right there." He stopped and pointed across the street to it. Roy stopped and looked where he pointed.

There was a nice looking old brick building with two large plate glass windows on the main floor with the door in the center and two little windows that you would see in a house on the second story.

"Oh, yes! I see it. Yes, that would be a perfect spot for us. Can we get inside?" Roy asked.

"Certainly, let's go." James said.

They walked a little faster across to the shop and stepped inside.

"This is just what we need. Why are you doing this?" Roy asked.

"I heard that you needed help. You have done so much for this town that I thought someone should extend a helping hand to you." He said. "Oh, by the way, the Mayor said to thank you too."

The comment about the Mayor flustered him, but he didn't let it get in the way.

"This is just what we need. How much will it cost for us to get into it?" Roy asked.

"It is empty now, so for you, there will be no down payment and no rent until the customers start to come. You can't pay for something until there is money. That's a business fact." James said and they both laughed. "You can remodel it any way you want to suit your business. What is your business anyway?"

"Donna is a florist and her family produces some of the best looking roses that I have ever seen. They live in New Castle over in Indiana."

"Now we will need to find equipment for the shop." Roy said.

"We're going to need a van to haul the equipment and the flowers and other things for the flower shop. I can't haul anything in my car." Roy said.

"There is a man at the paper that has a van for sale. I'll talk to him to find out the condition and price of it." James said.

"I know all the owners in town. I'd bet that I could find all the equipment you would need. Give me a list and a few days." James said.

"Could we buy the building and live in the apartment up stairs?" Roy asked.

"You want to buy it? You want to buy the building?" James said in a shocked voice.

"Sure. It makes good sense. I'm renting an apartment on the other side of town. We could live here and walk to work and my school." Roy said. "We could fix up the apartment and live there till something happens."

"Where is the school? I thought I knew all of them." James said.

I'm going to Newark Chiropractic College. It's right around the corner there." Roy pointed in the direction and James looked.

"So you're going to be a doctor?" James said.

"Well, I'm working very hard toward that end. It's not the easiest thing I have ever done." Roy said.

"Good for you! Do you know that we don't have a Chiropractor in this town now? You will have a monopoly." He said and they both laughed about that.

It didn't take long for James and Roy to settle on a price that sounded way too cheap to Roy, but James suggested it.

"You start on the cleanup and I will find the equipment and all the keys to the place." James said.

The price was right for the little van. It was an easy sell for Roy to get the van.

Roy and James got the contracts ready for the building and Roy bought it and made it ready for anything they might need it to do.

Now it was time for Roy to get back to school and get fitting into those grueling classes.

For the next few weeks, Roy and Donna spent all their time cleaning and painting with people coming and going every day. The people of Newark seemed to be very happy to see a flower shop about to be opened.

James found counters, a desk, a cash register, bathroom fixtures, a lot of little display things and a few people who would help with the paint. Roy thought there would be tile and carpet needed to put down on the floor of the shop, but after close examination, it was not needed. The wood floor needed to be sanded and stained, that's all.

It was nothing fancy, but it would work. With the energy both Roy and Donna and others would put into this project, it would be a winner.

The bathrooms were a different story. Remove and replace from the floor up. What fun. Roy had to hire a plumber for the bathrooms, both up and down, and he did a great job. But more tile and cleaning and painting was needed, both upstairs and down.

Once the apartment was finished, Roy took his new trusty van to their apartment across town and began hauling furniture to the apartment above the shop. He could only do one load per day after school. It took nearly two weeks, even with a little help from a few men friends to get it all moved.

The building was built in the early nineteen hundreds and there is a small one car garage in the back yard. Only one problem. It is too small to get the van into, a normal size car was too big to fit also. Roy's car would drive into the garage, but then Roy couldn't get out of the car. Roy hasn't inspected it closely yet, but it might make a good workshop.

After the place was ready for customers and the apartment was livable, Donna really got excited.

"I can put up curtains and pictures now." She said.

Roy smiles at almost everything that Donna says, this was a big smile.

Donna decided to put up a chain link fence around the whole lot. Roy has a two handle posthole digger known as 'the killer', but he really doesn't want to dig all those postholes with it. Roy rented a gas powered posthole digger with the big auger threads. It took him less time to dig all of them than it would have to dig just one with 'the killer'.

A dozen Rose of Sharon plants were planted around the outside of the lot with a walkway around the inside of them. The vegetable garden came next. The bees loved the Rose of Sharon and kept everything going and growing very well.

Roy's dad has an old rototiller, and Roy borrowed it to loosen up the dirt in the center where Donna's flowers and veggies will be planted.

Donna made raised beds of three by six feet inside the walkway. She wants lettuce, tomatoes, cucumbers, corn and green beans. Only one kind of vegetable to a raised bed. Donna knows where and when to plant each one. Good thing!

You should see Roy. When he gets home from school, he dons the old raggedy clothes and spends an hour with Donna in the garden. By that time he is drenched with sweat and exhausted. It is time for him to go inside and get composed and prepare to study the day's classes.

All the rest of the space in the garden was for her flowers. Most of it was on the level with the walkways, but some special areas were raised. Donna really knows her plants and she picked some that she would be using, selling and those that would grow in this area.

"A short list would be carnation, geranium, chrysanthemum, baby breath, gladiolus, daisy, snapdragon, purple statice, and lilies of all kinds. The roses were the most important to get planted." She said to Roy.

"There are a lot of specifics with roses. Where and when they should be planted is important. Roses need at least five hours of sun every day. Morning sun is best. And don't plant them close to a concrete foundation, because of the alkalinity." She said.

"Peat moss is a good thing, and you have to make it heavier than usual when planting. Keep the plants about twenty to thirty inches apart, and plant in the spring if you can." She said.

Roy is getting a mandatory class in roses today. When Donna gets like this he has learned to 'be still and know' is the best advice.

"One thing about roses is that they take a lot of care, but the rewards are extraordinary. And don't forget to feed them. A dose of seven percent nitrogen, seven phosphorous and seven potash mix is the best. The shop would only be selling Orchids on

Mothers Day. And you can't grow them anywhere around here." She said.

"The next thing we need to do, is to get a cat to take care of the birds, rodents and bugs that will want to eat my flowers and vegetables." She said.

"The cat will not be allowed in the house. You can make a very nice 'cathouse' for it under or near the back porch." She laughed out loud when she said it.

Donna spent the next several days selecting and planting vegetables for their meals and flowers for her store. Roy was only involved when she would ask, "What do you think," questions.

He generally doesn't have a good answer to that because he wasn't thinking about it.

Her parents came for an inspection and a delivery of a truckload of flowers of different kinds. Her mother and dad helped unload all the products into the big main cooler and the two little show coolers.

Customers must have been watching, because there were people in the shop examining everything before her parents had left.

'Blossoms' was open for business! And Roy didn't even know it.

Roy built a special house for the cat and Donna furnished it with good smelling towels and food and a little catnip. It was located right next to the back porch, but protected from any inquisitive dogs.

All the vegetables Donna planted were to be used in the salads and meals that Donna would fix every day for them. It's a good thing Roy likes vegetables. I think Donna forgot how to cook anything else for a while.

The flowers were mostly annuals since most of them have more color and bigger flowers available. Donna made a deal with her mother to have her send all the cut roses and a few rose bushes that she could, to Newark.

The heavy work was done and Roy and Donna hit the couches upstairs exhausted.

"Let's sleep for a week and then get started again." She said.

"I think that's a fine idea. While we sleep we should think what we want to do about the big party we promised everyone." He said.

"I forgot!" She yelled and sprung up from the bed to her feet.

"I have an idea. We could call a caterer and pay her in flowers. And just have an open house for anyone who wants to come." He said. "You just planted the garden, so we'll have to order more for the shop, make it a bigger order." Roy said.

"You think that will work?" She asked.

"No. But give it a try." Roy said and smiled a lot at his little joke.

Donna quickly picked up the phone and dialed a well known number.

"Mister Hamilton, this is Donna at the Blossoms. Do you have a minute?"

"Certainly, what may I do for you?" He said.

"I would like to have a big Grand Opening party here with drinks and snacks and desserts. But I don't know a caterer. And I don't want to do it when there might be something special going on around town." She said.

"I think I can help on all the questions. I know a very good caterer, they will get together with you to make a menu, and I will check for any conflicting dates." He said.

Early the next morning Donna answered the phone.

"Blossoms Floral. How may I help you?"

"Is this Donna at the Blossoms?" She said.

"Yes. Who is this?" Donna said.

"My name is Carol Webster. We are Webster Catering. James Hamilton called me and said you might want to have a party." She said.

"Could you come over here? I'd like to get started as soon as possible." Donna asked.

Donna and Carol Webster spent most of the morning going over the details of the Grand Opening party. It will be a big deal I think. I have to make sure Lucy is not involved.

Once the catering details were set and the date cleared, Donna called James to ask how to advertise this shindig.

"Let's make it an Open House where people can come in and walk around and meet you and Roy. I can do a half-page ad for you a couple of days ahead and you will be amazed at who will show up." He said.

Well he was right. They picked a Wednesday for the Grand Opening, and there were people in the shop before nine in the morning. The caterer had the best little hors d'oeuvres and snacks Donna had ever seen.

Both Roy and Donna's moms and dads were there. Their moms were glowing with pride and joy. They made their way around to each and every customer and greeted them warmly. But what the moms really wanted to see was the apartment upstairs. Donna was pulled away from the celebration and they hurried her upstairs to show them what they would be living in.

"Oh look! This is beautiful! Did you do the decorating here Donna? The colors are so pretty." Donna's mother said.

"Yes! I agree! Roy is certainly lucky to have you helping him." Roy's mother said.

"Did you know that Roy asked Donna to marry him?" Alice said.

"No! I didn't! Have you accepted, Donna?" Betty said.

"Yes, actually, I did." Donna said.

Both women suddenly forgot about looking at the apartment and wanted to hurry down to the shop and loudly congratulate Roy and tell the world that they were ecstatic. It took the trip all the way down the stairs for Donna to stop them and explain a few things to them and calm them down before they told the whole town.

Just then a customer walked up and asked. "Do you have any Cottage Roses?"

"Yes, of course." Donna said, relieved to get away from the moms. "Right over here."

She pointed toward the roses she had mentioned and the woman came to look. As she walked away she gave the out-of-control moms a look that would have melted a glacier, and they stopped and shut up.

"Would you like me to make you a gift arrangement?"

"Yes, that would be wonderful." The two women got together and made up the perfect arrangement for her.

Both moms quietly crept into the main room and found a seat.

The party went on without a hitch. Roy's younger sister kept count of the people who entered the store. Many of them bought something during that first day.

Much of the flowers that came with Donna's parents were sold and about half of the existing stock as well. It was a big day for the business.

By the time Roy returned from his classes, most of the people had thinned out and both mothers grabbed him and hugged him and whispered into his ears as they did.

"Why didn't you tell us about her?" Mom asked.

"I'm so glad she found you." The other mom said.

"Actually, I found her." He said.

"We're going to have a wedding, we're going to have a wedding." Both moms sung the words to themselves and danced to the words and music in their heads and whispered to each other and smiled and grinned. They both smiled for at least an hour afterward.

After all the prospective customers and friends had left, James and the two moms wanted to see the apartment upstairs. Alice led boldly as she usually does. She was almost running up those stairs to get to the beautiful apartment where her grandbaby would be born. She was excited, even if she had more than one thing confused.

"Mo - om! Would you slow down! All these things you are talking about are not going to happen to-day!" Donna said.

James looked and smiled at the apartment. "I never thought you could get it to look this good, Roy." He said.

"It took time and patience for this miracle to hap-pen." Roy laughed.

Roy's dad was the most pleased of all. He was the one who taught Roy how to build.

They all sat in the comfortable chairs and couches and Roy and Donna served wine and cheese to them.

"What are your plans now dear?" Alice asked.

"I will work in the shop, and Roy will finish his schooling. Once he is done, we will buy another of Mister Hamilton's buildings and locate the Doctor's Office in it." Donna said.

She couldn't help but laugh at her own joke. James and Roy also began to laugh. Soon they were all laughing.

"After Roy is finished with his training and he has his practice established, I will take a few courses in something, so that I have a trade to fall back on." Donna said.

Alice and Betty both stood up and said together one word by one word, "We would volunteer to run the shop for you while Donna is in school, if you want." They sound like Abbot and Costello.

"Don't you listen? After Roy has his practice established! We don't have the money for both of us to be in school at the same time now!" Donna said.

Alice and Betty sat down meekly and didn't say anything more. Grandmothers are strange.

The party was over and the people began to drift out and down the stairs. James was the last one out before the family. Roy and Donna thanked him over and over for all he had done for them.

"Don't forget Roy, once you get ready to buy another of my buildings, to call me." He said. The three of them laughed for several minutes about that and James left.

Now that everyone is gone, I must tell Roy about the news flash I just received.

"Roy Listen!" I said.

Roy doesn't usually acknowledge the voice in his head, but ever since the episode with the ring, he listens.

"You will soon have an opportunity to buy a piece of some very valuable land just outside of town for a very low price. Buy it when I tell you. It's important."

Chapter 35

More and More School

Roy is entering his third year at NCC, Newark Chiropractic College. Now that Blossoms and the apartment above are finished and usable, Roy has more time to study and his grade point average is going up.

Roy relished the month off between the Pre-Med at Ohio State and the first classes in October at MCC when he started his first year. But this year he is back on the regular schedule and he didn't have that big vacation.

Monday will be the first day of his third year. I know he is looking forward to it. That's a joke, folks.

Roy has already been through anatomy, physiology, chemistry, pathology and bacteriology. He worked very hard on chiropractic technique and X-ray. Practice management was one course that he studied the most.

Now he must work on caring for the patients and caring for the business. Probably the two most important phases of the whole course.

Roy has a slight advantage, since he played football, he knows about sports injuries. Roy will be making himself available to the Panthers and other teams around the area as their sports chiropractor.

He will be focusing on sports specific injury evaluation and treatment during the football season. And there will always be attention to the athletic emergencies common to football.

Since there is no other Chiropractor in Newark, Roy's business development will be pretty easy. But the school has plenty of classes that Roy will be intensely interested in during the year.

One early spring Saturday morning, George Martin walked into Blossoms and asked for Roy.

"He's in the back. I'll get him." Donna said.

"I was told that you were looking for a little place outside of town. My wife died recently and I have some acreage that I want to sell." George said.

"I would be glad to see it, if we can stop and get my dad to look at it too." Roy said.

The three of them drove out of town to see many acres of unused fields. Roy and his dad walked around the land and said that it was just fine if the price was right.

George told them a price that seemed to be very low for what they were looking at.

"There is two hundred acres here and I will sell it in pieces if you like. I will sell forty acres first and give you an option on another forty acres every six months until it is all sold." George said.

"Let's get to the bank right now. If they will finance me, we'll take it! Roy said.

I'm really glad Roy listened to me this time. It will be more good for him than he thinks.

Between friends, relatives, customers and phone calls, Donna finally got her garden planted and actually growing.

Roy has helped when his studies allowed it.

Soon the veggies started coming and Donna was elated. There was lettuce and tomatoes for a great sandwich. There was sweet corn and green beans for a great meal. And of course there must be cucumbers for pickles and slices into the salads.

Donna isn't a vegan, but she and Roy really loves the vegetables with any meal. But she needs roses!

During the Christmas break, Roy took the opportunity to contact Coach Miller and visit with him. They met at a little café on a side street off of the square.

Roy stood when the coach walked to the booth. The waitress took their orders and was back in a flash.

They both had coffee, but no food.

"Well Roy, how are you?" Coach said.

"I'm doing well." Roy said.

"I thought you were at Ohio State." He said.

"I did my Pre-Med there." Roy said.

"We saw you in the Rose Bowl. You were terrific." Coach said. "You're a doctor now?"

"Yes and I'd like to offer my services to the Panthers as a Sports Chiropractor. I know football and football injuries, and I think I could help." He said.

"I think you might have a good idea there. Let me talk to the Athletic Director. We don't have a doctor on staff now." Coach said.

Roy had business cards made up a few weeks ago with his name and Blossoms address and phone number.

"I'll be available after graduation and our office is completed, but before next season. Here's my card. I put the home phone on the back." Roy said.

"My wife would be the one answering the phone when you call."

"She's a florist? Blossoms. Oh, I know where that is. That's great! Sometimes we send flowers to someone in the hospital, or when they're hurt. We can use you from now on." Coach said.

"I'll need to find a receptionist once I get the office located and ready to begin business." Roy said.

"I know a man who is going to close his business and I'll bet his receptionist would be good for you." The coach said.

"Would you please tell her to call me?" Roy said.

The meeting with the coach went well and Roy was feeling good about it.

As the coach walked out, a man came to Roy's table and introduced himself. "I'm Martin Lowry, I represent a company in another state." He explained that he had been trying to find Roy for some time.

"You own a piece of land outside of town here don't you?" He said.

"Yes, I do." Roy said.

"I am interested in it and I would like to buy it." He said.

"Go on."

"I would be happy to offer you one million dollars for it." He said.

"Before we go any further, I would want to know that there is no criminal business involved in this transaction." Roy said.

"There is not. I am an agent for a large computer company. I wouldn't handle it if there were. I can't tell you the name of the company. I'm not allowed to do so." He said.

"Let's get the contracts to a lawyer so I can know what I'm doing. I don't have any trouble keeping a secret if it is not criminal or dangerous." Roy said.

"Good! I will have them to you tomorrow. Will the Blossoms be the place to deliver them?" He asked.

"Yes. That's just right." Roy said.

Roy spent the next week working on actual people, pretend patients, to help them feel better. For a few weeks, Roy and a couple others traveled to Columbus to a Chiropractic Clinic to help out with their patient load there.

The contracts were delivered to the Blossoms two days later. Roy looked at them, but not being a lawyer, he was ill equipped to know right from wrong. But he knew someone who did.

"Dad, who is that lawyer you always go to for help?" Roy asked.

"You remember William Roberts, don't you, the lawyer on North Third Street, and where his office was located?" Dad said.

"Yes. I remember him." Roy said.

Roy ran over there and asked the lawyer to examine and approve the contracts or tell him what to do about them.

It was a short meeting with William Roberts. Roy gave him the contracts and Mr. Roberts told Roy to see Ray O'Neill for help with the monetary side of things.

The next day Roy called Ray O'Neill, the Financial Planner recommended by lawyer Roberts. Roy explained what was about to happen and that they didn't want to lose a lot of the money to the Government for no reason. They set up an appointment for the next day after school.

"What did you have in mind, Roy?" Ray said.

"I just don't want to give the Government money they didn't earn." Roy said.

"Let's talk about Future Concepts Mutual fund. I think we can make this work very well." Ray said. "I'll get back to you."

Roy hurried back to school. He didn't want to miss a minute of any of it. There is so much to learn.

Roy worked most of the morning and all of the afternoon. He wanted to work on the hardest ones so he could learn more about the finesse of the job.

"It's not enough to know what to do to fix a pain or a soreness. It's about doing it right." Roy said.

Roy was becoming known as a perfectionist. Someone you can trust.

The semesters got longer and longer. There was more to do at home in the apartment and in the shop. Donna's Blossoms became more popular very day. Donna was concerned that her roses would not produce for a few months and she still must get her roses from her mom and dad.

Roy will soon have a trip to Zanesville to work in another Chiropractic Clinic. The same group of students who went to Columbus will be there together. It means that he will get more hands-on experience. And that's what he needs.

Lawyer Roberts called to say that the contracts were genuine and valid and there was money backing them. If Roy wanted to sell the land, he could do it at any time. The lawyer said he would be at the closing if they wanted him there. Roy called his dad and they talked about the land sale.

"Let's get this done!" Dad said.

"I agree! I'll call Roberts and Lowry to tell them to get a time set up and finish this." Roy said.

James has a habit of coming to the shop during the day. He happened to walk in as Donna was complaining. She usually doesn't do that very often, but it was hot that day.

"It's too bad we can't grow soda in cans." She said

"I think I know where there is a pop machine that you could buy and put in here." He said.

"Really? That would be great! The customers all want a drink when it's so hot like this. I want one every day." She said and perked right up.

James easily found a pop machine for them. Roy paid for it and had it installed. Donna and her customers were asking for it and happy to see it in the shop. It's amazing what a tiny little favor will do for someone.

"When we put this pop machine in here, I never dreamt it would sell out so often. I have to fill it once a week, but I love it." She said. "I'm going to put in a few chairs for people to sit in when they come." Donna said.

Roy was a busy little beaver. He had classes at the Chiropractic College. He had to help Donna with Blossoms almost ever day. He did the cleanup in the apartment upstairs every day, and he washed dishes and put them away.

He took time to study every day and kept up with the classes very well. But Molecular Biology, Organic Chemistry and Kinesiology were beginning to get under his skin.

The sale of the land went off without a hitch and Roy and his dad were presented with a Cashiers check for one million dollars. Roy and his dad followed Mister Lowry back to his office and finished all the necessary paperwork.

Roy and his dad were now co-owners of a mutual fund worth a million dollars and no tax was needed to complete the deal.

"Ray, I would like to talk to you about a house. Donna and I are living in the apartment above the Blossoms, but I know we are going to have children. I would like to find a nice three bedroom, two bath house and still keep the apartment for guests. Do you have a good contact I can trust?" Roy asked.

"Yes, I do. I'll call him right away."

"Hey Bill, I have a client who wants someone to find a house for him and his wife and soon to be family. Could you come over and talk to him?" Ray said.

Bill didn't ever wait too long to see a new client when they are standing somewhere waiting on him. It was only seven minutes till he drove up.

Bill Denning and Roy walked out to Bill's car as Roy told him what he wanted. They drove around a few of the neighborhoods and scanned the area and the houses.

"There! What about that one?" Roy said.

Bill stopped the car and found the right key and they walked around through the house at 1134 Arlington Street.

"This is just what I'm looking for. Can I afford it?" Roy asked. Roy doesn't want anyone to know about the land sale or the money. Because of that, he will always ask questions like that to keep up appearances.

They sat down at the kitchen table and went over the numbers and decided that with a little down, Roy could afford to buy it right away. So he signed the papers with an offer.

"I sure would like to show Donna the house. Do you think you could do that while I watch the Blossoms?" Roy said.

Donna loved it and the contract was submitted.

It took a few days for the offer to come back, but it was accepted and Roy and Donna had a nice house in one of the nicer areas in town.

"You know we have to paint every wall, don't you?" Donna said.

"Yeah, yeah, yeah. I know!" Roy said shaking his head in disbelief.

Donna spent an hour picking out the exact colors for the rooms in the new house. For the boy's bedroom, Dusky Cerulean Haze. That's a blue for those of you who, like me, didn't know. For the girl's bedroom, Primrose Pink. Easy. For the master bedroom, Lemon Chiffon. And for the kitchen, April Shower. The den is more modern with a Country Fog grey color.

Donna and Roy painted the house walls and she loved it more each day. Roy and his dad built a small one and a half car garage for the Mustang and Roy's tools. The van will be in use nearly every day.

It will take a few weeks to get furniture bought or moved into the house. Roy is looking ahead toward the wedding and all the people who will be swarming around them.

One big question that hasn't been answered in Roy's mind yet is this. Where will they go for a honeymoon? Roy doesn't know and he hasn't asked Donna yet. And He doesn't want anyone else to know. Quite a quandary.

Chapter 36

Doctor Roy

Roy's graduation was a big event for him and Donna, but there were others in attendance. The Clarks, the Spencers, James Hamilton and some of his people, Coach Miller, several of the other coaches and several friends were in the auditorium to witness the big event.

There weren't many students at this graduation since it was an off-schedule event. The normal class schedule is, as everybody knows, fall through winter and spring, ending in late May or early June.

But Roy started out off-schedule and didn't take the vacation breaks that the others did. He was in a hurry to finish.

Graduation day was finally here. Donna, the Clarks, the Spencers, James Hamilton, all were excited to see this day come.

I made sure to have a choice seat for this event. I didn't want to miss one second of it.

Mister Kimball, the Dean of the College was center stage in front of the podium. He introduced himself and told a little about the school and what they did. There were fewer students graduating today than a normal class. He introduced each one. Then it was Roy's turn.

"Charles Roy Spencer."

Roy stood and walked along the prescribed route until he met Mr. Kimball standing in the middle of the stage. He took Mr. Kimball's outstretched hand with his right hand and received the cardboard tube with his left.

"Congratulations Roy."

When Mr. Kimball released his hand, he spoke his name again and Roy made his way back to his seat. He reached up and moved the tassel to the left side of his cap. He was a College graduate! His return to his seat was a blur, but he made it. He graduated! Now he was a Chiropractor. A real doctor. A D.C. He even got a plaque for his wall.

"Are you ready to get married, my darling almost-wife?" Roy asked and laughed.

"Well Doc. Yes. Where have you been all these months?" Donna said also laughing.

"I already contacted the Methodist Church over on Church Street and the minister said he would do the service for us. We can use their hall for the reception." He said.

"I'll call Carol at Webster's Catering, she will be glad to do the cake for me." Donna said. "I even know someone who will bring flowers for us." She laughs at everything, even her own jokes.

"What are we going to do about Bridesmaids and the Best Man?" He asked.

"I've already got that covered." She said.

"Did you set the date?" He asked.

"Yes. We have two weeks." She said.

"But we can't do it that soon." He said.

"OK, make it three weeks, Superman." She said and laughed that laugh again. "I'll get the dress and all the people, all you have to do is put everything together and get the rings." She said.

Roy went shopping for rings. The first place he stopped was the pawn shop where he found the big ring, but no luck. He visited Taylor Jewelry and Mr. Taylor had just what he wanted. Roy brought them home with a big smile on his face.

Donna and her mother went shopping for the dress and Donna found one that was "perfect" hanging there on the rack just waiting for her.

"What luck! You don't find a size six white wedding dress on the rack, ever!" Mom said.

Luck indeed! I made sure it would be there.

During the time left, there were rehearsals and lunches and dinners and meetings. By the time everything was ready, Roy was exhausted. He wondered if he had the strength to stand up there and make it through the ceremony.

The stage was set and the time finally came for the big performance.

"We are gathered here today in the sight of God, to celebrate one of life's greatest moments, to unite Roy and Donna in holy matrimony." The Preacher began the ceremony.

"Shall there be anyone who has just cause why this couple should not be united in marriage, they must speak now or forever hold their peace."

There was silence in the church.

Charles Roy Spencer, do you take Donna Clark to be your lawfully wedded wife, to have and to hold, in sickness and in health, for richer and for poorer, to love, honor, cherish and protect her, forsaking all others, forever more?

"I do."

Donna Marie Clark, do you take Roy to be your lawfully wedded husband, to have and to hold, in sickness and in health, for richer and for poorer, to love, honor, cherish and protect him, forsaking all others, forever more?

"I do."

"By the power vested in me, I now pronounce you husband and wife. You may kiss the bride."

The minister then announced to the people. "I now present to you Mr. and Mrs. Roy Spencer."

"The reception will be held in the Fellowship Hall next door." The minister said.

Now that the service is over it was time for the bride and groom to share the first dance. The church pianist had taken her seat and began to fill the room with beautiful pleasant music.

Donna has whispered in Roy's ear. "I tested last week and I'm pregnant."

"That means we're going to have a baby!" His voice was louder and much more excited.

"Yes!"

Roy was elated. He jumped around and everyone thought he was doing a new fast dance out on the floor.

Donna got him under control and had him sit next to the wall for a few minutes while she danced with the fathers.

Lots of uninvited people came to the wedding. People who watched Roy play football, the football team, people from the college, and people who knew them through the flower shop. There were so many that most of them had to stand out side during the service.

And the Fellowship Hall was full to overflowing when Donna told the mothers about her pregnancy. They yelled and jumped around and made such a fuss that she had to herd them outside to talk to them.

"We'll handle the Blossoms shop while you go on your honeymoon." Alice said. "And we'll cover it when you go to the hospital to deliver our grand-child." Betty said.

"There are so many presents that we'll have to have a garage sale to get rid of them. Ha, Ha." Roy said.

The honeymoon was top secret. No one knew where they went or how they traveled. Actually, they both ducked out of the Fellowship Hall unobserved a few minutes early. They wanted to be on their way before anyone could follow them. Roy and Donna enjoyed a very long weekend from all the distractions of life. They were alone together and loving it.

The first day that Roy and Donna was back to work. She opened the Blossoms and Roy called James.

"Now that I have graduated from the College, I will need a place to locate my practice." Roy said.

"I think I have just the right building for you." He said.

"Wonderful! That would make my day! Where is this building?" Roy asked.

"The building is on the square around the corner to the right." They stepped out the door and James pointed across the street to it. Roy stopped and looked where he pointed.

"Oh, yes! Yes, that would be a perfect spot for us. I can't walk to work in the morning anymore, but this will be perfect for what we want." Roy couldn't see the building from there, but he knew where it was. "Can we get inside?" Roy asked.

"Certainly, let's go." James said.

They walked a little faster across to the building and stepped inside.

"It looks like this is just what we need." Roy asked.

"It is empty now, so for you there will be no down payment and no rent until the customers start to come. You can't pay for something until there is money. That's a business fact." James said and they both laughed.

"I have heard that somewhere before." Roy said.

"You can remodel it any way you want to suit your business." James said.

"Now we will need to find equipment for the office, and a sign for the front." Roy said. "I have catalogs that the school let me use."

"Could we buy the building?" Roy asked.

"You want to buy it? You want to buy this building too?" James said.

"Yes. Well, we do have the money now." Roy said.

"What money?" James asked.

"I sold a large piece of property that I had out east of town." Roy said.

Roy contacted Ray O'Neill about buying the building and Ray suggested a plan that James and Roy found to be acceptable.

"We will wait until interest and capital gains are posted before we pay it off. Is that alright with you?" Ray asked.

"That sounds good to me." James said.

But now they had another remodel program on their hands. They had to make a waiting room with chairs and end tables and lamps. They had to make exam rooms with all the special equipment. They had to make a supply room to keep all that special equipment in. They had to make a main office and a private office with desks and chairs.

The worst of all was the apartment up stairs. And the same as the Blossoms building, the upstairs bathroom was the biggest headache. Roy and the plumber sweated and strained on it for three days and finally finished it.

But it all got done because Roy stayed with it and hired the right people at the right time.

The special equipment was delivered by UPS and FedEx on exactly the right day and was put in its place.

The coach was as good as his word. He found the receptionist he told Roy about and she showed up during the remodel. She would be ready to start work on the first day the office was open.

The sign company hung "Spencer Chiropractic" in big letters over the door, and Roy was open for business.

During the next few weeks, Roy had the first few customers in his office. He also had meetings with the Athletic Director and Coach Miller. The AD agreed to buy the necessary equipment for the team. He didn't want any injured player to be transported downtown for an exam or treatment. Roy agreed to be on hand during games if he could bring family members.

The Athletic Director agreed and said that he would assign a separate box just for the Doctor and his family so they would know exactly where the Doctor would be if needed.

Donna and her parents and Roy's parents all said it was wonderful what he was doing for them and others.

The deal with the big computer company in the sky was completed some time ago and Roy and his dad worked for weeks on where to put the money.

A million dollars! Give a hundred thousand to Dad, give a hundred thousand to the Salvation Army. Get with James Hamilton and the Nutrition center, the food pantry, a hundred thousand in the bank for Donna.

The Financial Planner, Ray O'Neill, had to stop them. "You guys aren't thinking correctly. There are ways to do this and ways not to do it. You two are on the wrong path. Let me show you how to get this right. Ray spent the next hour drawing pictures and writing numbers on his board until they both said, "OK, I think we understand now."

"Let's get everything signed and legal before we leave here today. There will be no questions now." Ray said.

Roy and his dad signed and finished the transfer of the money to the mutual fund.

"Thank you for not letting us throw all that money away. And the recipients will like it a lot more I think." Roy said.

"I've got to buy a better car, and Donna needs a car too. This little Mustang is just not going to work for me anymore. But I'm going to keep it!" Roy said. "How do I get the money for that, Ray?"

Ray found a way to withdraw enough for Roy and Donna to buy newer cars. Not new cars. Donna wanted something that they could drive to her parents home in Indiana. Roy wanted something to drive when they go out to dinner with friends.

Ray made a deal with the Ford dealer for a pair of three year old Lincolns. Roy and Donna were elated about the cars.

Roy had a strange call from the Newark Police.

"Did you have anything stored in a safe deposit box in the bank, Sir." He said.

"Yes I have box number ninety nine and there is a big ring that I bought for my wife in it." Roy said.

"Could you come to the station, please." He said.

"Certainly. I'll be right there." He said.

Chapter 37

Let's Have Kids

After the robbery at the bank, the police questioned all the people who had property stolen. When they got to Roy, they were surprised at the item he described to them.

"It is a big ring. It has a full carat diamond in the center, surrounded by a circle of sparkling emeralds, and that is surrounded by a circle of emerald cut amethyst, and a circle of small ten point diamonds around the outside, all mounted in twenty two carat gold." Roy said.

Mister Taylor here knows much more about it than I do." Roy said.

"There is a necklace of the same design with it. The necklace was designed to wrap around the neck and hang down to the breastplate. There was also a large red ruby solitaire at the bottom of the necklace. But it's missing." Mister Taylor said.

"I have done some research on the crown jewels." Roy said. "The complete set has a tiara with it. It has many diamonds and rubies in it. I would estimate the whole set to be worth millions. No one has seen it in many years. The set of jewelry was a gift from a King of Jordan to his queen centuries ago." Mister Taylor said.

"If you want photos of the ring, I will give you what I have." Mister Taylor said.

The police thanked Roy and moved on to the next person.

For Roy the wedding was the best thing ever. But when Donna and Roy danced that first dance and she told him she was pregnant, he about jumped out of his skin. He was so happy he couldn't contain himself. Donna saved him by sitting down with him for a few minutes.

To make sure he sat seated, she placed herself on his lap and told him she would talk sweetly to him if he calmed down and sat there quietly until she returned. Which he did.

The honeymoon was even better now that he knew a baby was on the way. Now they must decide on a name for a girl and a name for a boy. Donna and Roy don't know what the baby is yet. Donna has appointments already set up with the doctor, so they will know soon.

"If we use a name from our grandparents, we could have James Philip and call him JP. The girls name could be Virginia Ellen. We could call her Ginny." Donna said.

"I think they should be close together in age when they go through school. They could help each other. Maybe two years apart would be good." Roy said.

"You want two?" Donna asked.

"I would love to have a boy and a girl, as beautiful as you." Roy said.

"The worst thing about being pregnant is that I'm tired all the time. I just don't want to do anything. Now with all this nausea and constipation to go along with being tired all the time, it's just been a barrel of laughs." She said.

Donna was still able to work in the Blossoms shop, but Alice and Betty visited daily. And Donna took advantage of their time and their energy.

"Do you know when it happened?" Roy asked.

"I know exactly when it happened, I even know which day it was, that first day in Zanesville, when we went shopping. Think about it, do you remember that day?" She said.

"Oh yeah, I remember! That day might go down in history as one of the most memorable days ever. But, how did you get pregnant that night and not before with all the sex we were having?" Roy said.

"I started using birth control pills when I knew you were the one." She giggled. "I knew that we'd be doing some kinda sexy things and I wanted to be protected if you didn't turn out to be the one." Donna said.

"You rat."

"I was using a backup every time we did anything. I stopped using anything the morning of the wedding and stopped taking my birth control pills before that." She said.

"You wanted to get pregnant?"

"Yes, I wanted to have your child, this will be something that you can look at every day and see me. One day you can say, 'I made that', and I'll be able to say 'I put the icing on it'." She said.

As time crept by for Donna, she learned more and more about the strains of having a baby and all the surrounding problems.

"Do you know what that doctor told me? 'Nausea during pregnancy is associated with good fetal health.' It may be good fetal health, but it sure is making me fetal bad. More constipation and abdominal pressure and discomfort than I ever thought possible. And I'm gaining weight like there's no tomorrow." Donna said.

I can't believe it! She made a joke.

Alice and Betty were becoming more involved in the Blossoms by the day. It won't be long before they will be forced to take over all the day to day work, since Donna will be laid up for the duration.

"Ow! Ow! That hurt! Do you want to feel the baby move? Put your hand right here." She said.

It's time for Donna to go to sleep and the kid decides to do a tap dance on her belly button. That girl is going to be a good dancer.

"Just think how good you'll look after the baby comes and you take all the extra weight off." Roy said.

He's trying to make her feel a little better about herself and her pregnancy, but it isn't working.

"Remember last month when you said I could look at her every day and see you. How right you were. Won't it be great if she does look like you?" Roy said.

"Don't forget, it could be a boy." She said.

"No, I'm convinced that it will be a girl and she will be the exact duplicate of you. And you will teach her all your tricks about how to bewitch and confuse the male population." Roy said.

"I just hope that I don't have trouble with hemorrhoids and varicose veins. I don't think I could handle them right now." She said.

Dad came over early the next day to help in any way he could. Roy was busy doing something downtown. When Roy arrived back home, dad already had everything under control.

"Hi Dad. Is Donna feeling OK today?" Roy asked.

"Yes, but she is having a bout with what the doctor calls 'Breathlessness'. She has trouble getting enough oxygen. He gave her some exercises to do, maybe they will help." Dad said.

"When I got home, Donna wanted to talk, we sat on the couch in the living room and she talked for hours. I don't know why, maybe I'll never know, but I love the sound of her voice and the sight of her smile, they always make me feel good inside." Roy said.

"She wasn't smiling when I arrived, but after she unloaded some of her problems, she began to smile again. It's been three hours, we've had lunch, or dinner, or something and she's talked the whole time, and now she's smiling that big smile she's known for." Chuck said.

Excuse me, I need to talk to Roy for a minute.

"Roy I want you to find the ruby and the three other pieces of the crown jewel set right away. I forgot to mention that there is a pair of earrings with the set. I know where they are hidden and I know who stole them from you and the others. I have a client who is a policeman who will help you. His name is Tom Baker." I said.

"You will meet him at the corner of Ninth Street and Western Street. The jewels are hidden in the basement of a church near there. They are in an old wooden trunk under the stairs and covered with cardboard and rags."

"The two of you will find them and you will call the police to come before you enter the building and take the police to where the jewels are hidden. The police will open the trunk and return them to the rightful owners. The owners in turn will provide a reward to both of you. You may use the reward in any way you wish." I said.

Officer Baker called dispatch to report that he and Roy found the stolen jewels and a lot more. Once the trunk was uncovered and brought into the light, they found a large cache of stolen articles hidden in it.

Placing the blame may be difficult, but it appears that a member of that church is the culprit. But the police did find one very nice fingerprint on the center of the big red stone.

"We will find the owner of that fingerprint very soon." Officer Baker said.

The police contacted the royal family of Jordan and they sent an envoy to pick up the jewels and deliver a large reward to the two men who found it.

The next day, Roy took Donna to another appointment with Doctor Hughes.

He took her home and by the time he pulled into the driveway in back she was smiling a little smile again and her color was beginning to come back. I was glad of that.

They walked in the back way and Donna collapsed on the couch in the living room.

They sat on the couch and Roy held her for another half hour, when out of the blue she began to cry.

"I seem to cry over everything." She said.

"What were you crying over this time?" Roy asked.

"Because I can't make love to you and won't be able to for several months." She said.

"That's not something to cry about." Roy said.

She finally began to smile when he said that. It grew a little and in a few minutes she was chuckling, then even a little laughing after that. She giggled about that for nearly an hour after that. She was feeling pretty good by the time Alice and Betty stopped by.

After the fingerprints came back, the police found that an employee of the bank was the one who stole the jewels. No one in the church was involved. The bank employee is now in jail awaiting trial. The whole town is mad at him. He may be in jail for a long time.

Roy remembered what the doctor told him months ago,

"Your job is to notify me and get her to the hospital with time to spare, after that, just get out of the way till I call you." He said.

"I've been going to Doc Hughes since the first day I arrived in town, and when Donna and I were dating, I took her to him just so she could decide if she wanted to change." Roy said.

Roy sat in the waiting room for thirty or forty minutes waiting for the doctor came out to see him.

"It was pre-term labor, Roy. I gave her some labor-inhibiting drugs to stop it. I also administered medicine to hasten the maturation of the infant's lungs, the crucial factor to the infants survival is the lungs ability to work properly."

"If the lungs fully develop in the next few weeks, and this happens again, we shouldn't have as much to worry about as we did this time." Doc said.

"Is the baby going to be OK now?" Roy asked.

"Yes, we're out of the woods on this one. Be sure she gets good nutrition from now on, she doesn't smoke, so that's a plus." He said.

"Is Donna going to be OK now?" Roy asked.

"Yes, she is resting comfortably, but that won't last long. I want her to stay the night and I'll look in on her tomorrow. What about you?" He said.

"I guess I'll stay till she can go home. I have some money and I'll call the moms, so I'll be OK." Roy said.

"Good, see you in the morning." Doc said.

Lucy is working very hard on this one. Donna is suffering because of him. I have made sure the baby is in good condition, but it's hard to keep up with both of them.

"Donna has had so many problems with this pregnancy and put on so much weight that the doctor told her not to go back to work till after the birth and he gave me a letter detailing all of it that I was to deliver to her boss." Roy said and gave it to Mom.

Roy has said to me so many times that he is glad that his mom and Donna's mom are helping with the Blossoms.

During the week Donna complained of headaches, swelling and gas pains. But the one thing that got her the most was, "I have to pee all the time." She said.

The baby is growing very fast and the extra weight and the baby moving around a lot is wreaking havoc on her body. When the baby sits on her bladder just right, Donna winces.

Donna and Roy were watching the Chiefs play the Steelers on TV when the doorbell rang.

Donna is so big now that she doesn't even try to get up for something like this. Roy answered the door and showed two of Donna's friends, Linda and Sandy, in to a seat on the couch, Roy took a seat in a chair off to the side while they talked.

"How are you feeling?" Linda asked.

"Terrible. Feel the baby kicking. He says it's a girl." Donna said pointing at Roy.

The doctor's visits seem like they are every day now, and delivery is right around the corner.

Roy was talking to Annie in the waiting room as the doctor examined Donna.

"The baby will come when they damn well feel like it so don't get too excited about it, just do what Doctor tells you." Annie said.

"You forgot my toiletries, I need a toothbrush, toothpaste, comb and brush and some cologne, get the gold bottle on the second shelf. And I need a pair of small pajamas, better make it two." She said.

Roy put the suitcase in the van so he didn't have to worry about forgetting it again.

Roy put her to bed at nine and stayed up for the news and weather on channel ten. Nothing new here, they're still predicting six to eight inches of snow tonight. He'd better get some sleep, it's going to be a long night.

At one thirty in the morning Donna kicked Roy out of bed and screamed, "It's time!" He called the doctor and rushed her to the hospital in the van. He thought it would be better if she laid on the floor of the van, the streets are slippery and he didn't want her falling or bumping anything.

It was very tough driving, He slid around almost every corner, some of them felt like he went through the corner twice. Fortunately there were no cars on the streets except Roy. He did a one-eighty at a corner that looked pretty safe. He had to stop completely and get the van turned around after that little bit of fun.

Roy's taking it really slow at twenty miles per hour, but the wind is blowing hard and the streets are extremely slippery. Roy executed a very nice three-sixty at the corner of two four-lane streets, and she screamed at him, "Are you trying to kill me?"

Roy drove up to the door and almost before he could stop, they were outside opening the side doors on the van and taking her inside on a gurney. He managed to park it and find his way back inside. He knew this was the real thing so he just went to the nurses station and identified myself and told them where he'd be waiting.

He found a semi-comfortable chair in the waiting room till he could go back to the labor room. It was only twenty or thirty minutes before a nurse came out to show me where she was. He followed her back to find Donna all smiles.

"What is this, she's still pregnant and she's smiling?" Roy said.

"The doctor said I was dilated enough to make it a natural birth and the delivery room should be ready in a few minutes. Come and hold my hand. Are you going to be here?" Donna said.

"Of course. All night if necessary. I'll be in to see you as soon as they'll let me." Roy said.

It only took another half an hour in the labor room before they moved her.

"Why don't you find a chair, Dr. Spencer? It could be a couple of hours. Someone will find you when we need you." One of the nurses said.

It was just coming up to five in the morning when Doc Henderson found him rereading everything in the waiting room.

"You were right. It's a girl! No wonder there were pains, the baby is 20 inches long and 9 pounds 2 ounces. Come on, you want to see her don't you?" Doc said.

They had baby Virginia cleaned up and Donna was holding her when the Doc and Roy found her.

What a sight! A one hour old baby is something to behold.

With her mother as beautiful as she is, it'll be hard to break the mold, she will be too. Would he like to hold the baby?

"What I'd like to hold is the mother and she can hold the baby." Roy said. They held each other for several minutes that way.

"Donna, I love you more than anything in this world." Roy said.

"I love you too, Roy." She said.

She kissed him! A real kiss, not just one of those pecks on the cheek or lips he's been getting for the last few months. The first time she has done that in a long time. It looks like she'll recuperate just fine. I sure hope so.

Roy and Donna have had more fun with that Mustang hot rod. Since they both have a more family oriented conservative car, they don't get to drive around and act crazy in it very often. Babies aren't comfortable in a fast moving race car. Roy has decided that instead of him getting rid of it, he should store it in the garage for future use. Good idea.

Chapter 38

A Good Life

Roy never was a big kid when he was growing up. He was picked on by the older, bigger boys, and sometimes girls too. There could have been lots of trouble in school from elementary all the way through high school, but his attitude was the deciding factor. He didn't enjoy making trouble. He made many friends though.

He was told he couldn't play football by an older student, but a coach told him differently, and he became the star of the show. Funny how people will lie to you just for fun.

He studied the required courses at a college for some time. It was difficult and he wanted to quit, but that word is not in his vocabulary.

A woman entered his life. In his words, the most beautiful woman in the world. His joy was through the roof. He couldn't have been happier than when they were married.

Roy had an old house that was not worth much, but it was his. He was always fixing it. It was a good thing that his dad taught him all he knew about carpentry and masonry.

Roy worked a long time on the house. He got it fixed up and sold, so he could buy a bigger better house for his wife and kids.

Donna surprised Roy at the wedding with the news of her pregnancy. The birth of Virginia Ellen

Spencer was very painful for Donna, but also extremely joyful for both of them. I fought with Lucy for the whole nine months to keep him away from Donna. It was hard, but we won that one.

Soon there would be another battle. James Philip Spencer was born two years and two months after Ginny with out much pain and suffering. Roy went on to become an excellent doctor and Ginny ran the family flower business.

Donna jokingly said that she could have another baby as soon as Roy wanted one. Both Roy and Donna knew that it was a big joke and Donna was done with being pregnant. There was a lot of laughing between those two about that.

Donna is now back on her feet and running around as if she was a teenager. Roy is loving it and her every day.

The Blossoms flower shop is doing well. It is a gathering place for many of the downtown women to come and have coffee and soda and conversation. Donna put in a few chairs when the pop machine was first installed. She soon realized she needed more chairs and a few tables. Then a coffee pot and cookies, then a counter with stools. Now Donna has a coffee shop in her flower shop, and all the women love it.

Now that Roy is a Doctor of Chiropractic, and the kids are out of the baby stage, Donna is going to Midwest Business College to get her degree in Business Administration. She probably knows as much as any of the students or teachers about the subject, but she still needs the paperwork that says she knows it.

Roy was a football star in high school and college, but it still took him lots of time to get his life on track. He has plaques and pictures on the walls of his office from the Cotton Bowl and the Rose Bowl and the Panthers at the State Championships.

Roy never talks about himself or his accomplishments. He is very proud of his kids and what they have done for the business, the town and the state.

Finding Donna was the best thing that happened to him. She made him what he is. There are special pictures of Donna at the wedding and pictures of his children. They adorn all the walls of his inner office.

I did help a little with the plot of land and the crown jewels, but Roy did all the work, I only pointed him in the right direction.

Possibly the biggest thing about Roy that helped him through life was that he was polite and gracious to everyone he met. A smile will melt the heart of even the meanest person if it's done right.

James was talking to the Athletic Director of the Panthers at the high school. The AD asked him what he thought of Roy and this is what James said.

"The true success of a man is measured by the gentleness of his touch, the kindness in his heart and the love he shares with his family." James said.

Roy's kids made quite a name for themselves. Ginny took over the Blossoms when Donna hurt herself and was unable to get around like she could before. But Donna did come to the shop for coffee and cookies every day and keep the women who came there company and entertained.

Roy's practice grew over the years and he especially enjoyed taking his friends and relatives to the Panthers football games.

When James Philip (JP) graduated from high school and went on to college for Political Science, Roy was flying high. Now JP is a US Congressman for the state of Ohio, and Roy is so excited.

"It's been a good life." Roy said.

"Yes, my darling husband. It's been a good life." Donna said.

Chapter 39

St. Nicholas

"Roy, I'm Nicholas Tanner. I am here to tell you a little story. Let's have a seat, this will be a long story and you might get tired of it."

I told Roy the whole story of his life and he was shocked. He doesn't know what to do now. None of the others knew what to do either until I explained everything to them.

"You must be careful not to talk to, or listen to, Lucy. It is vital to your survival."

"What do you mean, you don't know who Lucy is? The guy in the red pajamas with the horns. He can look like anyone he wants, man or woman. He can also look like any animal as well. Unfortunately, I always see him as he really is. Not a pleasant sight, but I have put up with it for centuries."

"Every time I call him Lucy, he gets mad. If I do it well enough and he gets mad enough, he disappears. Then I have a little time without his interference. Good times!"

I told Roy about the opportunity to buy a certain piece of land really cheap. He didn't want to spend the money, but I finally convinced him that I was on his side. He finally did the sale a little later.

Later, the land sold for a million dollars to a computer company that wanted to build an assembly plant in the Midwest. I explained all I knew about the crown jewels and how I helped him find them.

"I would like to tell you that your dad asked my boss to keep an eye on you. That's how I got this job."

"I thank you for everything you have done for me and our family and our town. I especially thank you for Donna." Roy said. "She is the love of my life."

"Goodbye Roy. I'll be watching you, and remember, where there no peace, there is no power."

I had to stop him. I can't listen to all this mushy stuff, so I just left.

Many years ago, I found a page in the trash with these words on it.

Nothing in the world can take the place of Persistence.

Talent will not.

Nothing is more common than unsuccessful men with talent.

Genius will not.

Unrewarded genius is almost a proverb.

Education will not.

The world is full of educated derelicts.

Persistence and determination alone are omnipotent.

I don't know who said this, but he was right. I hope we showed what persistence can do.

Most of us spend our lives seeking our destiny. It began in a manger and led to a cross and it included

you. You too have a destiny and someday - - - someday soon, your destiny will cross with his.
    Daniel Firman